THE CASE *of the* VANISHING PAINTING

BRIAN GALLAGHER was born in Dublin. He is a full-time writer whose plays and short stories have been produced in Ireland, Britain and Canada. He has worked extensively in radio and television, writing many dramas and documentaries. Brian is the author of four adult novels. He has written many books for young readers, including: *One Good Turn* and *Friend or Foe* – both set in Dublin in 1916; *Stormclouds*, which takes place in Northern Ireland during the turbulent summer of 1969; *Secrets and Shadows*, a spy novel that begins with the North Strand bombings during the Second World War; *Taking Sides*, about the Irish Civil War; *Across the Divide*, set during the 1913 Lockout, *Arrivals*, a time-slip novel set between modern and early-twentieth-century Ontario; *Pawns* and its sequel, *Spies*, set during Ireland's War of Independence; *Resistance*, an alternate history set in a Nazi-occupied Ireland; and *Winds of Change*, set during the Irish land wars. Brian lives with his family in Dublin.

THE CASE of the VANISHING PAINTING

BRIAN GALLAGHER

THE O'BRIEN PRESS
DUBLIN

This edition first published 2024 by
The O'Brien Press Ltd,
12 Terenure Road East, Rathgar,
Dublin 6, D06 HD27, Ireland.
Tel: +353 1 4923333; Fax: +353 1 4922777
E-mail: books@obrien.ie
Website: obrien.ie
The O'Brien Press is a member of Publishing Ireland

ISBN: 978-1-78849-391-8

Layout and design by Emma Byrne
Cover illustration by Dermot Flynn

1 3 5 7 6 4 2
24 26 25

Printed in the UK by Clays Ltd, Elcograf S.p.A.
The paper in this book is produced using pulp from managed forests.

The Case of the Vanishing Painting receives
financial assistance from the Arts Council

Published in

Dedication

To Max, with much love.

Cast of Characters

Deirdre Kavanagh, *twin sister of Tim.*
Tim Kavanagh, *Deirdre's twin.*
Mr Kavanagh, Deirdre and Tim's father, *guard on the Galway to Dublin train.*
Mrs Kavanagh, *Deirdre and Tim's mother.*
Joe Martin, *Tim's best friend.*
Mr Martin, Joe's widowed father, *a clerk in the railway company.*
Charles Wilson, *a director at the National Gallery of Ireland.*
Sadie Nolan, Maura Breslin, and Beth Breslin, *local girls.*
Superintendent Leech, *police officer leading the investigation into the art theft.*
Con Furlong, *captain of a trawler.*

PART ONE

Accusations

CHAPTER ONE

Iona Road, Dublin

FRIDAY 9 JUNE 1911

Deirdre Kavanagh had never committed a crime before. And if she got caught now, breaking into someone's house, she would be in huge trouble. *So make sure you don't get caught.* Because this was something she simply had to do for her father. Although Da – law-abiding, peaceable, and honest to his core – would be horrified if he knew she was breaking the law for him.

Deirdre knew, though, that she must put all that from her mind and keep her wits about her. She could feel her heart pounding. Mostly it was from fear of being discovered, though there was also a tiny hint of excitement at what she was doing.

She quickly scanned the study of the comfortable suburban house, eager to complete her mission and escape. The house was richly furnished, with polished mahogany bannisters on the stairs, deep pile carpets throughout, fine paintings on the walls, and a beautiful piano that Deirdre recognised as a Steinway. Even to a twelve-year-old it was obvious that this was the home of someone with money and taste.

Although she had a good reason for being here, she couldn't help but feel slightly guilty for invading another person's privacy. *Forget that*, she told herself, *concentrate on what you're here for*. What exactly she might find though, was hard to pin down. Evidence of some kind, clues to indicate that the owner of the house was involved in crime. But what precisely that might be she couldn't say.

Deirdre understood that the owner of the house was unlikely to leave something incriminating in open view, but she still had to look for any hint of wrong-doing, any clues that might be of use. *You'll know what you're looking for when you see it*, she reasoned as she went to examine the folders that were on the desk before her.

Quickly scanning through them, she saw that they contained notes about holiday schedules for staff at the National Gallery, travel and accommodation expenses for a recent trip to Galway, and dates, times, and list of exhibitors for a planned art exhibition. Nothing about any of them seemed suspicious to Deirdre, and she moved swiftly on, aware that every moment spent in the house added to the risk of being caught.

Her brother Tim was keeping watch in the road outside, and Deirdre had arranged that he would blow a football whistle to warn her if she needed to get out quickly. They had waited until the housekeeper had left to do the morning shopping before Deirdre had climbed the rear wall and gained entry to the back garden. It was a hot summer day, and Deirdre had guessed correctly that a kitchen window might be left open to let some cool air into the house. Entering through the downstairs window, Deirdre had quickly explored the empty house. She had decided that the study was the room most likely to provide clues to the owner's activities, with the room full of files, ledgers, and notebooks.

The problem was time. The housekeeper had gone out with a shopping basket, but there was no way of knowing if she would be back soon after buying one or two items, or if her shopping trip would be more leisurely. *And if she came back too soon…*

Deirdre forced the thought from her mind, aware that if she gave way to fear it could paralyse her. Instead, she tried to concentrate on her task. She looked at the owner's desk and read with interest a letter that lay open there, then she tried the top drawer. It wasn't locked, and Deirdre opened it and saw that it contained an address book. She took it out and scanned through it. Deirdre had an excellent memory, and she trusted herself to memorise anything that might strike a suspicious note. But the names and addresses, written in neat, round, handwriting, all seemed to be either business contacts, or people – presumably friends and acquaintances – with addresses in the wealthier districts of the city. *Which doesn't rule out the possibility of them still being criminals*, she thought.

Nothing struck Deirdre as being noteworthy, however, and she closed the address book, making sure to replace it exactly where she had found it. At the side of the drawer was another smaller book, and Deirdre took it up. Opening it, she realised that it was a planner, with names, dates, and times of appointments, written up in the same neat hand. She was scrutinising entries for the current month of June when she saw an entry that caught her attention. She paused for a moment, reflecting on it, then heard a sound that stopped her dead. A loud whistle blast had rent the air. Deirdre felt a stab of terror and she stood immobile. *The housekeeper was returning.*

Deirdre could feel her stomach tightening into a knot. But she couldn't just stay here and be discovered. Moving quickly, she replaced the planner and shut the drawer. *Please, God, let me not be caught*, she thought. She strode across the study, hoping that she could swiftly descend the stairs and exit from the kitchen before the woman entered the house. She reached the landing and moved to the top of the stairs. Then she heard the sound of a key in the hall door.

Deirdre stopped, rooted to the spot in horror. For a second, she stood unmoving. Suddenly her survival instinct kicked in, and she did a fast about-face and reached the safety of the study just as she heard the front door opening.

Deirdre stood motionless inside the study. Her breath was coming in short bursts, but she knew she had to calm herself and try to think clearly. The housekeeper was likely to bring her shopping into the kitchen, which meant that Deirdre couldn't exit from the house the way she had entered. Could she chance descending the stairs at speed, and getting out the front door while the woman was in the kitchen? Maybe. It would be risky, but she might get away with it. Then again if the housekeeper heard the front door closing she would probably investigate immediately – and see Deirdre walking away from the house.

Deirdre heard the woman stepping into the hall now and closing the hall door behind her. Suddenly a new thought entered Deirdre's head. What if the housekeeper didn't go immediately to the kitchen. What if she came upstairs?

Frightened as she was, Deirdre was clear in her mind about one thing. *She couldn't let herself be arrested.* Da was already in enough trouble, without his daughter being brought home by the police. She strained her ears and heard the sound of the woman's footsteps going down the hall, then the kitchen door being opened and closed.

Deirdre felt a flood of relief. She knew though that her reprieve was temporary, and that there was no guarantee the housekeeper would stay in the kitchen. Deirdre thought again about quickly descending the stairs. If she went out the front door – but didn't close it after her – the woman might hear nothing. And what of it if she later found the hall door slightly ajar? By then Deirdre could be walking innocently down the road.

It wasn't a perfect plan, but it was the best that Deirdre could come up with. She took a deep breath, trying to get her nerve up for the risky act of descending the stairs. She was just about to move off when she heard another sound from down below. Deirdre stood stock still as she heard the housekeeper moving back along the hall. She prayed that the woman would enter one of the other rooms downstairs. Time seemed to stand still as she waited to see what would happen. Then her mouth went dry, and her knees began to tremble, as she heard the housekeeper beginning to climb the stairs.

Four days earlier

CHAPTER TWO

GREAT WESTERN SQUARE, DUBLIN

MONDAY, 5 JUNE 1911

'We need to talk, Joseph.'

Joe Martin had just finished a juicy slice of apple tart and he pushed aside his plate and looked across the dinner table at his father. Nobody except Dad ever called him Joseph, and he much preferred the more informal Joe, but he could hardly tell his father what to call him. Joe had been looking forward to returning to the Sherlock Holmes detective story that he was engrossed in, but now he would have to postpone that pleasure.

'OK, Dad,' he said. Although he was eager to resume reading, part of him was curious about what it was his father wanted to discuss. Dad wasn't normally a great one for talking, so this was unusual.

'It's eh…it's a little tricky, Joseph,' he said, looking uncomfortable.

Joe knew it must be something important for Dad to raise an awkward topic. He loved his father, who was decent and kind, but sometimes Joe wished that he wasn't so reserved. But then Dad had never been good at showing his feelings – even before Mam had died. After the heartbreak of her death, though, Joe had thought he and Dad might form a closer bond. But in the three years since then Joe had had to accept that Dad hadn't really changed. He looked at his father now and tried to help him out.

'Whatever it is, Dad, just tell me.'

'It's Tim. Tim Kavanagh.'

'What about Tim?'

'I know you're good pals, and he's a nice boy, but…'

'What?'

'I think it might be wise to step back a little, Joseph. Just for now.'

'Step back?'

'Perhaps not see him too much. Until this theft business has been sorted out.'

Joe was shocked by his father's suggestion. The previous week there had been a sensational art theft when the train from Galway to Dublin had been transporting valuable paintings back to the National Gallery after an exhibition. The most valuable of the paintings had somehow gone missing between the train leaving

Galway and arriving in the capital. Tim's father, Mr Kavanagh, was the guard on the train, and along with the driver, fireman, and three mail clerks, he had been questioned by the police.

'Ah, Dad!' said Joe. 'You don't really think Mr Kavanagh was involved?'

'No, Joseph, I don't. But it's not what I think that matters. This reflects badly on the Midland Great Western Railway. Management are most unhappy.'

'Yes, but…'

'The newspapers are having a field day, Joseph. The police are in a tizzy. So, the whole company is under a cloud. I have to think of my position, for the sake of our family.'

Joe knew that his father put a high value on the fact that he was a white-collar worker in the Midland Great Western Railway's Headquarters at nearby Broadstone Station. The houses in the Great Western Square complex had been built for employees of the railway, but there were deliberate differences in design, with general workers like Tim's dad living in a terrace of smaller houses while Joe and his father lived in a larger house that had a pocket garden in front. Joe thought that such distinctions were foolish, but he knew his father – and the railway company – took these things seriously, so he had to go carefully here.

'I know, Dad, that the robbery was awful. But I thought that under the law you're innocent until proven guilty.'

'Well, yes, that's true. But…'

'But not Mr Kavanagh?'

'Don't put words in my mouth, Joseph. I told you I don't doubt Mr Kavanagh's honesty. And this would only be until this issue is sorted out.'

'What happens if it's not sorted out? Supposing they never catch the thief?'

'We must hope and pray that's not the case. It's just…this is a difficult time, Joseph.'

'Is that not when a true friend should stand by his pal?'

Joe looked appealingly at his father. In fairness to Dad, he had always had a strong sense of justice, and Joe hoped that his arguments might have swayed him.

Dad looked torn, then seemed to reach a decision.

'All right, then. You don't have to break off contact with Tim. But be discreet, Joseph. Tim's father is certain to be questioned further. So when it comes to the Kavanaghs, try to keep out of the public gaze, all right?'

Joe looked at his father and felt a surge of affection for him. 'All right, Dad,' he said. 'And…and thanks…'

* * *

Golden evening sunshine flooded the backyard, the heat of the June day lingering in the air. The puffing of a steam train approaching Broadstone station drowned out the earlier sound of birdsong, and clouds of smoke from the •

the blue summer sky as Tim Kavanagh and ⅃

on a bench in their small backyard.

'This feels like rubbish!' said Tim, putting down

lyrics written on it. 'I can't concentrate. I can't make th⅃

'I'm the same,' said Deirdre.

They were supposed to be working on a comedy song that t⅃
were to perform with their friend Joe Martin at the annual Great
Western Square residents' concert, but Tim breathed out in frustration. 'It feels kind of silly now,' he said. 'Compared to what's
happening with Da.'

'I know,' agreed Deirdre. 'I hate the way they're acting like he's
a thief. I mean, anyone who knows Da could tell you he's dead
honest.'

'They don't care,' said Tim. 'They just want to arrest *someone* for
the stolen painting.'

'Did you know that when the train reached Dublin they didn't
just question Da, they searched him too?'

'What?'

'Like he was a pickpocket or something,' added Deirdre
disgustedly.

'Did Da tell you this?'

'No. You know him, he's bending over backwards to shield us.
But I heard him talking to Ma before he left, and he's worried
sick.'

n felt really bad. His father had gone fishing in the Royal
.al, and Tim suspected that it was to give him a break from
tting on a brave face.

'It's so unfair,' he said. 'People who don't know him could think
he's a thief now.'

'That's not his biggest worry,' said Deirdre.

'No? What is?'

'He said to Ma he was afraid he could lose his job.'

'They can't do that!' said Tim immediately.

Deirdre didn't answer, and Tim looked at her enquiringly. 'Can
they?'

'Who knows?'

'Surely they'd need proof to sack you for being a thief.'

'You'd think so. But maybe if there's a question mark over your
good name they could decide they don't want you working for
them.'

'I wish they'd just catch the thief and end all this,' said Tim.

'Me too. But we can't do anything right now, so we should
probably try to work on the song.'

'All right. I wonder what's keeping Joe?'

'He said he'll be here, so he will be.'

Tim nodded as he picked up the lyrics again. Deirdre was
right, and Tim knew he was lucky to have a friend like Joe who
was always as good as his word. In some ways they were unlikely
friends. Joe was strong and sporty, and the star of their school's

Gaelic football team. Tim by contrast was slightly built and not very good at sports. But both boys loved reading, and the combination of being bookworms, close neighbours, and the same age had made them firm friends.

'I wonder would the sketch work better if I did the song in a different accent?' said Tim, studying the lyrics again.

Deirdre considered for a moment 'Well, you brought the house down when you did the Scottish accent at last year's concert.'

Tim knew he was good at acting – it was what he wanted to do when he grew up – but he looked at his sister uncertainly. 'Or maybe that would feel like we were repeating ourselves.'

'Look who's coming,' said Deirdre. 'Why don't we ask himself?'

Tim looked up from the lyrics as the back door opened, then Joe stepped out into the yard.

'Sorry I'm a bit late.'

'It's grand, sure you're here now,' said Deirdre.

'What kept you anyway?' asked Tim.

'I was doing a bit of thinking,' answered Joe, a hint of excitement in his voice. 'Maybe you'll say I'm mad, but I've had this idea that…I think you should hear.'

'OK, Joe,' said Tim with a smile. 'You've whetted our curiosity. What is it?'

* * *

The back door swung open, and Mrs Kavanagh stepped out into the yard carrying a tray of mugs of milk and plates of soda bread smothered in jam.

'Refreshments for the *artistes*!' she said jokingly doing a French pronunciation on *artistes*.

Joe grinned in return, recognising that his friends' mother was striving to keep things normal despite the tension that he knew the family was under. He liked her outgoing personality, and he appreciated the way she treated him almost as though he too were one of the Kavanaghs. Partly it was to do with him being friends with Tim and Deirdre. Joe suspected though that it was also rooted in kindness, and her awareness that although on two days a week a housekeeper prepared meals and cleaned the Martins' house, living with just his father could sometimes be lonely.

Joe hadn't had a chance to share his big idea with Tim and Deirdre, but he was happy enough to wait a little longer if it meant enjoying Mrs Kavanagh's home baking.

'Rhubarb jam. Mouth-watering, if I say so myself!' she said.

'Thanks, Mrs K,' answered Joe, 'it looks great.'

'Let me at it,' said Deirdre. 'After strawberry jam, rhubarb's my favourite.'

'Don't scoff it all, greedy-guts,' said Mrs Kavanagh.

'As if I would,' answered Deirdre playfully in a pious voice.

All of the friends took their mugs of milk and slices of soda bread, then Mrs Kavanagh paused before heading back to the kitchen.

'On a serious note,' she said, her face suddenly grave.

'What?' said Tim.

'Did you hear about the accident at the jam factory?'

'No,' said Joe.

'Nothing could be preserved!'

'Mam, that's terrible,' said Deirdre in mock protest, but she was smiling, and Joe laughed with Tim despite the joke being silly. He knew that Mrs Kavanagh must be worried about her husband, and he admired her for trying hard to keep life normal for her children.

After she went back inside, closing the door after her, the three friends eagerly tucked into the jam-covered soda bread.

Tim wiped a tiny moustache of milk from his upper lip, then turned to Joe. 'So, you were about to tell us your mad idea?'

'Yeah...' Joe paused, unsure how best to proceed.

'Well?' prompted Deirdre.

'All right,' said Joe. 'Believe it or not, it started with the latest Sherlock Holmes book you lent me. I love the way Holmes' mind works. And it got me thinking.'

'About what?'

'About the art theft. And how Holmes might try to solve it. I thought...I thought maybe we could try to do that.'

'Find out who stole the painting?' asked Deirdre.

Joe could hear the disbelief in her voice, and he quickly held up his hand. 'Please. Don't get me wrong. I'm not treating this like a game. I know it's serious for your family.'

'OK,' said Tim. 'But…what would we do?'

'If we discovered who the thief was, it would clear your da's name. And the other people who are under suspicion.'

'That would be brilliant,' said Deirdre. 'But if the police can't do it, how could we?'

'Maybe by thinking in a way the police don't think.'

'How do you mean?' asked Tim.

'I wrote it all down – everything I know,' said Joe, taking a piece of paper from his back pocket and unfolding it. 'So let's go through what we have, and lay out the facts.'

'All right,' said Deirdre.

'So am I right that there were three mail clerks, a driver, a fireman, and a guard – your da – working on the train that night?'

'Yes,' answered Tim.

'And there were three passenger carriages?'

Tim nodded. 'Two second-class carriages and one first-class. Mr Wilson, the man from the National Gallery, travelled in the first-class carriage.'

'But no one else from any passenger carriage would be allowed into the guard's van,' said Deirdre. 'And that's where they sorted the mail and stored the paintings.'

'So the people who *could* go in are the staff working on the train – the three mail clerks, your da, the driver and the fireman.'

'And the station-master in Athlone where they stopped to take on water,' added Tim.

'All right,' said Joe. 'And Mr Wilson, the Director from the National Gallery, supervised the loading of the right number of crates of paintings into the guard's van?'

'Yes,' said Deirdre. 'Our da and the three mail clerks all saw that.'

'Fine,' said Joe, lowering his notes. 'So what it boils down to is that the paintings were put onto the train leaving Galway, and when the train reached Dublin the most valuable painting was gone.'

Tim nodded again. 'The police reckon one of the workers on the train has to be the thief. Mr Wilson checked all the paintings when the train arrived in Dublin, and he called the police the minute he found that one frame was empty. He made sure all the staff on the train were questioned, and searched, before they were allowed to leave the station, and nothing was found.'

'But the painting can't have vanished into thin air,' said Joe.

'No,' said Deirdre. 'But how are we supposed to see it in a different way to the police?'

'That's where the Sherlock Holmes thing got me thinking. Holmes claimed that when you rule out the impossible, then whatever you're left with must be the truth, however unlikely it seems.'

'Yes, I love the way he does that,' said Tim. 'But how do we do it in this case?'

'If the painting was gone when the train arrived in Dublin,' answered Joe, 'and none of the staff had it, and it didn't vanish in thin air, what does that leave?'

Deirdre and Tim looked thoughtful, then Deirdre shook her head. 'Sorry, Joe, I can't come up with anything.'

'Me neither,' conceded Tim.

'The only explanation is that it wasn't on the train *leaving* Galway.'

'But…but that doesn't make sense,' said Deirdre. 'We know it *was*.'

'How do we know?' asked Joe.

'Mr Wilson confirmed it.'

'Exactly,' said Joe. '*Mr Wilson confirmed it.* But nobody else actually saw the painting in its crate on the train in Galway. We've only Mr Wilson's word.'

Joe could see that Tim and Deirdre were taken aback.

'But…why would he lie?' asked Tim.

Joe looked his friend in the eye. 'Why do you think?'

'You're not saying…that he robbed the painting he was in charge of?' said Tim incredulously. 'Da says he's a director in the National Gallery – it would be like robbing himself.'

'But he wouldn't be robbing himself. He'd be robbing his employer. And the fact that it seems unthinkable is the clever part. He makes himself the victim of a crime, and makes it seem that one of the train staff must be the thief. Why would the police think the unthinkable? Why would it occur to them to suspect a highly respectable Director of the National Gallery, someone who raised the alarm in horror, and seemed the *victim* of a crime?'

'It's…it's still pretty outrageous,' said Deirdre.

'It is,' agreed Joe. 'So it's much more likely that the police – and everyone else – would jump to the wrong conclusion.'

'My head is reeling,' said Tim.

'Mine was too when it first hit me. But no other answer fits all the facts, and this one does.'

'So, what can we do?' asked Deirdre.

'Take it on as a case the way Holmes does. We could look into this Mr Wilson. What do you think?'

There was a pause as Tim and Deirdre looked at each other. Joe said nothing further, figuring that it was their decision.

'If there's any chance of clearing Da's name, we should do it,' said Deirdre.

Tim nodded. 'Absolutely.'

'So, the three of us take it on?' said Joe.

'Yeah, count me in,' said Deirdre.

'Me too,' added Tim.

'That's settled then,' said Joe. 'Let's check out Mr Wilson.'

CHAPTER THREE

'Train, train, number nine,
Run along a crooked line,
If the train goes off the track,
Do you want your money back?'

Deirdre listened to the skipping rhyme, then timed her move perfectly, stepping under the skipping rope and jumping easily each time it spun down towards her feet. The local girls often played street games at the entrance to Western Square park, and Deirdre now jumped in tandem with Sadie Nolan, one of her classmates from school, while two other girls, Beth and Maura Breslin, swung the skipping rope and chanted the rhyme.

Classes had finished for the summer the previous week, and there was still an air of novelty about being off school that had the girls in good humour. Though they were neighbours and class-mates, Deirdre had never really liked Sadie Nolan, who tended to talk about people behind their backs and to play off one friend against another. Still, Mam always said that everyone in life was on the same journey, and that we should try to get on as best we can with anyone we met.

Although it was only ten o'clock in the morning the air was warm already, and the bright June sunshine held the promise of a hot summer day. Despite the cloud hanging over her father because of the art theft, Deirdre felt better this morning than she had in the six days since the painting had gone missing. Partly it was the sunshine and the summer holidays stretching in front of her, but also she felt energised by the decision made last night with Joe and Tim to start their own investigation. Deirdre wasn't as keen on detective stories as Joe and her brother were, but the fact that they were planning to take action had given her a lift.

This morning the boys had left for the library as part of their mission. Initially Deirdre had intended to go with them. Joe, however, had pointed out that while they needed two people to carry out their plan at the library, the less they exposed themselves to public view the better, and that it made sense to save Deirdre for other parts of their investigation.

She was eager to hear how they got on, but knew that there was nothing she could do for now. Instead, she tried to immerse herself in the pleasure of skipping and she chanted the rhyme as she skilfully skipped.

After a while the girls agreed to change places, with Beth and Maura handing over the rope for Deirdre and Sadie to swing. As they took up their ends of the rope, Sadie turned to Deirdre. 'You must be dead worried,' she said.

'About what?' answered Deirdre, although she sensed from the other girl's smug expression that this had to refer to Da's situation.

'That your father might end up a jailbird,' said Sadie.

Deirdre felt a surge of irritation, made worse by the tone of false concern that Sadie had adopted.

'My father is as honest as the day is long,' she answered, keeping her temper in check.

'Still. He was the guard on the train when the painting went missing,' said Sadie. 'Who knows how that could end?'

Deirdre saw that Beth and Maura had heard Sadie's comments and were waiting to hear her response. Her instinct was to let rip and put Sadie Nolan in her place. She knew, though, that Sadie's father had a more senior role with the Midland Great Western Railway than Da, and that to make enemies of the Nolans wouldn't be a smart move. At the same time, she couldn't let Sadie make little of her father.

'Who knows how any of it could end, Sadie?' she said keeping her voice calm. 'But if they don't catch the real culprit, it damages the Midland Great Western Railway. And that would be bad for all of our fathers. So, if you want to worry about something, worry about that.'

Sadie looked unsure what to say, and before she could come up with an answer, Deirdre raised her end of the skipping rope and turned to Beth and Maura.

'OK, girls,' she said. 'Let's skip!'

* * *

Tim breathed in deeply, both to calm himself and to savour the aroma. He loved the smell of libraries, and today the heat of summer warmed the still air of the library and heightened the scent of old books. Normally he found it relaxing to browse in the library, but now his pulses started to race. He glanced over at Joe, and although his friend looked calm, Tim suspected that he too was feeling nervous. For their plan to work their timing had to be spot on. Still, there was no reason why it shouldn't be. Both he and Joe were members of the children's section of the library, and they also frequently brought books back to the adult section for their parents, so they were familiar with the layout.

Tim hesitated briefly just inside the entrance door. Then he took another deep breath, and walked as confidently as he could towards the counter. Joe followed right behind, and both boys placed books for returning on the polished counter.

'Good morning, Miss Quinn,' said Tim to the librarian, speaking in the hushed tones that were expected in the library.

'Good morning, boys,' she answered, also in a lowered voice.

Despite the warm weather Miss Quinn was dressed as usual in sensible clothes. She was a heavy-set, middle-aged woman whose appearance was a little forbidding, but Tim had found that she was actually helpful and encouraging to anyone with a love of reading.

The librarian checked their books in, then Joe spoke politely. 'I wonder if you could help me, Miss Quinn,' he said.

'In what way?'

'I'm doing a project about the River Nile, and I was hoping you could show me where there are atlases or encyclopaedias I could study.'

Tim found himself holding his breath again. For their plan to work Joe had to distract Miss Quinn, but if she stayed behind her desk, they would have a problem. Tim already knew that the encyclopaedias were in a far corner of the children's section of the library, and they had deliberately come early, so that things would be quiet in the library and Miss Quinn would be more likely to leave the counter.

'Did school not finish last week?' she said, looking Joe in the eye.

'Yes, it did.'

'Then how come you're doing a project?'

Tim's heart skipped a beat and he saw Joe hesitate fractionally. Then his friend gave his most charming smile and raised his hands to Miss Quinn, as if in surrender.

'I know it makes me sound like a bit of a swat,' he said. 'But it's just a project I'm doing for myself. I love geography.'

Tim watched the librarian carefully, trying to gauge if she had bought Joe's explanation. She seemed to consider for a moment before speaking.

'Never apologise for seeking knowledge,' she slowly said. 'The idlers and the corner boys may mock you. But knowledge is the key to advancement, and you'll have the last laugh on them. Follow me.'

Yes! thought Tim, though he kept his face impassive as the librarian rose from her seat and came around the counter.

Joe followed Miss Quinn as she made for the far corner of the children's section, but Tim held back until she was out of sight. Moving briskly, but not so fast as to draw attention, he slipped into the adult section of the library. There were few people here this early in the morning and Tim avoided eye contact with those who were browsing. He knew his way around the adult library from having come here with Ma over the years, and he made his way directly to the reference section. Tim reckoned that he could count on Joe to keep Miss Quinn distracted for a while, but all the same he would have to carry out his task quickly. He scanned the reference books on the shelves. There were more than he expected. How long had he got? It was impossible to tell. But if Miss Quinn came back and saw him the game would be up. *Forget that, and concentrate on what you're doing.* He forced himself to continue scanning the shelves, but to no avail. And then he saw it. A red, leather-bound book with Thom's Directory on the spine. Tim glanced around to make sure that nobody was watching him. Then he slipped the book under his jumper and walked back towards the children's section.

To his relief, Joe and Miss Quinn were still around the corner, presumably organising atlases and encyclopaedias. Tim swiftly took several books at random off the shelves, then sat at a table, took the Thom's Directory from under his jumper, and covered it with the other books.

He opened one of the books and pretended to read it, then after a moment he saw Miss Quinn approaching, followed by Joe, who carried two encyclopaedias and an atlas.

Joe raised an eyebrow in enquiry, and Tim gave him the tiniest of nods, then smiled at Miss Quinn as she passed on her way back to the counter. Joe sat at the table spreading out the atlas. As planned, he sat with his back to Miss Quinn so that even if she looked over towards the two boys she wouldn't see what Tim had in front of him.

'Well?' said Joe in a soft voice.

'Took a while, but I got it,' answered Tim, sliding the directory out from under the other books. Thom's was a well-known listings directory detailing property and owners throughout Dublin, and he opened the book and began to leaf through it. He could feel Joe's eyes on him, but he concentrated on his task.

'Any luck?' said Joe anxiously.

'Not so far,' answered Tim, then he suddenly stopped turning the pages. He felt a flutter of excitement in his stomach, and he looked at his friend.

'Got him?' said Joe.

'Got him.'

'What does it say?'

Tim checked that Miss Quinn wasn't looking in their direction, then he spoke softly. *'Charles Wilson, graduate of Trinity College Dublin, and the London School of Art. Acquisitions Director of the National Gallery of Ireland. Member of the Kildare Street Club.'*

'Is there an address?'

'Yes. He lives on Iona Road.'

'Iona Road?' said Joe, unable to keep the excitement out of his voice. 'That's not all that far from us.'

'No.'

'That will make checking him out that bit easier.'

'Let's hope so,' said Tim. Now that they had gained information on their suspect he felt strangely torn – partly excited, yet partly afraid that maybe they were clutching at straws. But if there was any chance of helping to clear Da's name he had to take it. 'OK,' he said, turning the opened page towards Joe, who had a pen and paper at the ready as part of his phoney River Nile project. 'Let's get his details down. Then we'll go after him.'

* * *

The sweet smell of mown grass carried on the evening air, and a refreshing breeze blew as the heat from the June day finally waned. The citizens of Dublin had thronged to Phoenix Park – one of the largest public parks in Europe – but now people were making their way homewards, on foot, by bicycle, and in horse-drawn carriages that lazily clip-clopped along.

Passing the imposing statue of Lord Gough on the park's main road, Joe and his father walked towards the North Circular Road Gate.

'Well played tonight, Joseph, your batting was excellent.'

'Thanks, Dad.' Joe felt that he *had* played well in the junior cricket match, but it was good to hear it from his father. Dad was always broadly encouraging, but he didn't give false compliments, which made it all the better when he used a word like excellent.

'Overall, your bowling is solid too, but maybe we could do a little work on your spin bowling.'

'That would be great, Dad.' Sport was one of the few areas where he and his father really seemed to connect, and Joe liked the idea of them working together to hone his bowling skills. Growing up in Limerick, Dad had apparently been a talented cricketer, and despite Joe's initial reluctance to take up the sport, he was glad now to be following in his footsteps.

The Christian Brothers who taught Joe were hugely enthusiastic about Gaelic football and hurling, but regarded cricket, tennis, and rugby as 'garrison games' and therefore too British for their tastes. Dad, however, had insisted that if Joe were to play Gaelic football for the school, he must also be a junior member of the cricket club.

Although Joe had never said so to his father, he recognised that Dad could be a little snobbish, and that as a white-collar worker he regarded cricket as a more socially acceptable pastime. Being a natural athlete, though, Joe loved sports in general and he wished that adults were less bothered about things like garrison games and what sports were suited to their social class. He knew that people regarded his father as a bit stand-offish. And although Dad was always courteous and helpful to the neighbours, with the exception of singing in the choir in St Peter's church, he didn't get involved in the local community the way other children's parents did.

They walked now by the boundary railing that enclosed the manicured lawns of the Peoples' Gardens, and Joe turned to his father. 'When will we work on the bowling, Dad?'

'Well, I have to work late on Friday night, and I have choir practice on Thursday. Perhaps tomorrow night?'

'Great,' said Joe. He was meeting Tim and Deirdre tomorrow for a picnic and to talk about the next steps in their mission, but he would still be back in plenty of time. Thinking about their investigation, he decided to push for some information. 'About the art theft, Dad,' he said.

'What about it?'

'Have the police made any progress?'

'Superintendent Leech and his team don't share their findings with me, Joseph.'

'Still, everyone at Broadstone must be talking about it.'

'Unfortunately, they are.'

'And what are they saying?'

Dad turned and looked at Joe, who hoped he hadn't pushed too far.

'It's an appalling crime, Joseph. Don't think it's in any way glamorous, or start taking a morbid interest in it.'

'I'm not, it's just…'

'Just what?'

'Like we were saying before, it's very worrying for Mr Kavanagh.'

'For Mr Kavanagh, certainly. But also for everyone else in the company. You do recall what I said to you on the topic?'

'Yes. I can stay friends with Tim and Deirdre, but I'm to be discreet until this is sorted out.'

'Precisely. So, see that you do, Joseph, all right?'

'All right, Dad.' But Joe had no intention of giving up on their secret investigation, and he walked on into the summer dusk, his mind on tomorrow's meeting, and how they might pursue their quarry.

CHAPTER FOUR

Deirdre carefully balanced the mug of cocoa on the tray as she exited the kitchen door and stepped into the backyard. She crossed to Da who was sitting on a chair in a corner of the yard that was lit by the morning sun. Her father was reading a newspaper and puffing on his pipe, but Deirdre wasn't fooled by the image of a man who was relaxing. Da had been summoned to an interview later this morning in Broadstone, with the police superintendent who was leading the art theft investigation. Although he was playing it down, Deirdre could tell that he was nervous about it, despite being totally innocent.

'Will you look at this,' said Da, lowering his newspaper and indicating the drink. 'You have me spoiled!'

Deirdre laid the tray on his lap, then indicated a plate containing biscuits. 'Brought out a few biccies as well, in case you feel peckish,' she said.

'Where would I be without you?' said Da, holding his pipe in one hand and raising the mug with his other. He sipped the cocoa, then smacked his lips. 'Lovely!'

Deirdre smiled, pleased to have lifted his spirits even for a few minutes. Making cocoa for her father had become something of a tradition between them. When Deirdre had been about seven she had done it first, excited to be able to make a treat for Da, and in the intervening years she had kept it going, as a little father and daughter ritual that they both enjoyed.

'Good luck later this morning,' she said.

'Thanks, love. I'm sure it will all work out fine.'

Deirdre knew that he was trying to shield her from worry, and she felt a sudden surge of affection for him. 'I think you're great, Da,' she said. 'And they should be able to see that too.' She reached over and kissed him on the forehead, and he lowered his mug, slipped his arm around her and gave her a hug.

Deirdre breathed in the comforting smell of her father, a combination of the scent of his hair oil and the aroma of the tobacco in his pipe, and she held onto him for a moment.

'Go on now, or you'll be late for your picnic,' he said, gently releasing her. 'I'll be grand, don't you worry.'

'All right, Da. See you later.'

'Bye, love.'

Deirdre stepped back into the kitchen where Tim was waiting. Tim called out the back door in farewell to Da, then they both picked up their picnic lunches from the table. Ma had gone to the local shops to get the daily messages, but she had packed two lunches for the twins, and Deirdre sensed that her mother was happy for them to be gone from the house on what could be a challenging day for Da.

After Joe and Tim had replaced the Thom's Directory at the library yesterday, and shared the information on Mr Wilson, the three friends had agreed to reflect overnight on what the next move should be in their investigation. And now Deirdre was eager for everyone to share their views. 'OK,' she said, 'let's call for Joe.'

* * *

The sunlight glinted on the surface of the River Tolka, and the faint humming of bees could be heard on the sweet summer air. On the far bank of the river Deirdre could see where the Botanic Gardens boundary adjoined the expanse of Glasnevin Cemetery, but on this side of the sparkling water it was untouched countryside. They had found a grassy bank for their picnic, and had swum in the Tolka, with Deirdre beating the boys as they raced upstream. She was a keen member of a swimming club, and she enjoyed outpacing Joe and Tim, thanks to her superior swimming technique, even though Joe was stronger and generally more athletic than her.

Deirdre now licked the last sticky remnants of rhubarb tart from the greaseproof paper in which it had been wrapped. 'All right, time to stop stuffing ourselves and get to work!' she said.

'OK,' said Joe. 'Well, we've had time to think things over. Who wants to go first?'

'I haven't figured it all out,' said Tim. 'But one thing struck me. When was the painting actually stolen? Because if it *was* Mr Wilson, he must have done that thing magicians do.'

'What's that?' asked Joe.

'Deirdre, remember we saw the magician at the fair last year, and we were trying to work out how he did that trick with the noose?'

'Yes, but we didn't figure it out.'

'But we did decide that he'd done the trick much earlier than people thought. So when he was giving us a chance to change our minds on which noose to put around his neck, it didn't *matter* which one they chose. He'd already worked his trick by only having fake nooses. Mr Wilson must have done the same. Before anyone went near the Galway train, he must have already stolen the painting.'

'But the painting was mounted in a large wooden frame – and that was definitely loaded onto the train,' said Joe.

'Then he must have taken the picture *out* of the frame. Maybe he rolled it up and then put it in a smaller container.'

'One of the things I thought about was how he might have got it to Dublin,' added Deirdre. 'Supposing he didn't want to bring it on the train, but he did roll it up smaller? Couldn't he *post* it? Directly to his home on Iona Road?'

'I never thought of that,' said Joe.

Tim looked doubtful. 'But think of it from a thief's viewpoint. Posting something leaves a trail. He'd have to show his face at a post office in Galway. And the stolen goods would have his address on it. Not to mention the chance of something that valuable going missing in the post.'

'So how did he move it?' asked Deirdre.

'Well, nobody was going to check his suitcase. He could have rolled the painting up. Put it between his clothes, and then put his suitcase on the train. When he cries out in horror that the painting has been stolen no-one dreams of looking in his own suitcase.'

'That makes sense,' agreed Joe.

'I think we have to look at it through the eyes of a thief,' continued Tim. 'What would *you* do in his shoes? Not just how do you get it to Dublin. But if it's to be sold abroad how do you get it out of the country? Where do you hide it in the meantime?'

Deirdre didn't answer immediately as she gazed out over the river, but her mind was wholly on the problem. 'If it was me, I think I'd bury it,' she said.

'That could work,' said Joe. 'My suggestion was going to be that we tail this Mr Wilson. But maybe first we should check his garden. See if there's any sign of something recently buried.'

'We could do that,' said Tim. 'But if it was me I wouldn't bury it.'

'Why not?' queried Deirdre.

'Supposing the neighbours see you digging?'

'They wouldn't see you if you did it at night,' she answered.

'But they might hear you. And wonder why you're digging in the dark of night. Or a fox might unearth it. No, I think if Wilson is our man he wouldn't bury it. He'd lie low for a bit, and not do anything to draw attention.'

'And then what?' said Joe. 'If we were the thieves – then what?'

'Then you sell the painting.' said Tim.

Joe shook his head. 'I haven't a clue how you'd go about doing that.'

'But you might know if you worked in the National Gallery, mightn't you?' said Deirdre.

'True,' agreed Tim.

'We need to learn a lot more about this Mr Wilson,' she said. 'And I…I have an idea about that.'

'What?' said Joe.

'I wouldn't normally suggest this. But Da's good name is at stake.'

'So what are you suggesting?'

'We need to do more than tail Wilson. And we need to do more than look at his garden. I think…I think we need to get into his house.'

'What, *break in*?' asked Joe.

Deirdre nodded. 'Yes. If that's what it takes, then I say we break in.'

T im stood immobile on the landing. There was a creaky floorboard outside his bedroom door, and he was careful not to stand on it and draw attention to himself. He knew that eavesdropping on a private conversation wasn't nice, but this wasn't a normal situation, and he felt justified in listening in on his parents who had left the kitchen door ajar downstairs.

It was early in the morning on the day after their picnic, and Deirdre was still asleep. Tim had just stepped out of his bedroom, but when he heard what his parents were discussing he stopped dead and closed the door over quietly.

'If I get sacked, Eileen, we could…we could end up without a roof over our heads,' his father said. Ma worked part-time in a fruit and vegetable shop in Phibsboro, but Tim knew that her pay wasn't a living wage, and he was unnerved by his father's comment. Da and the other train staff from the night of the robbery had been under a cloud – especially Da as the guard – but it hadn't occurred to Tim that if Da lost his job, and was no longer a railway employee, they could lose their home.

'You won't be sacked,' said Ma.

'We don't know that. I've already been questioned twice. And now Superintendent Leech and Mr Wilson want to interview me again tomorrow.'

This was news to Tim. But disturbing as it was, another part of his brain was thinking that if Mr Wilson and Chief Superinten-dent Leech were interviewing Da, it would be a perfect time to gain entry to Wilson's house.

'They're not just interviewing you, Brendan,' said Ma. 'Every-one's been called back in – it's not like they're singling you out.'

'Not yet. But they might.'

'That would be totally unreasonable.'

'Maybe. But there's no telling how this could turn out. They'll want to convict someone – you can be sure of that.'

'The union won't let you be sacked and put out of this house. There's not a shred of evidence against you.'

'I know that, Eileen. But innocent men have gone to prison before. And if I got convicted of a crime, being in the union won't save me.'

'That hasn't happened. So let's not cross our bridges till we come to them,' said Ma. 'Just make sure you tell the police *exactly* the same story every time you're questioned, all right?

'I will.'

'And I'm sure that in the end the truth will come out.'

'Let's hope so,' said Da. 'Let's hope so.'

Tim stood unmoving on the landing trying to weigh up everything he had heard. He had known all along that Da had been shielding him and Deirdre, but he hadn't realised just how much his father was worried. Tim wanted to believe his mother's positive take on things, but supposing she was wrong, and Da was right? It made the task of checking out Mr Wilson all the more urgent. Still, there would be a window of opportunity tomorrow when Superintendent Leech and Mr Wilson were interviewing the railway workers. It meant that Wilson would be gone from the house on Iona Road, and if Tim got the time of the interviews from Da, that would be the moment to search the Gallery Director's home. Feeling more determined than ever, Tim breathed out deeply then started down the stairs.

* * *

'How did you pick the piece for Sunday's concert?' asked Mr Martin, wearing what Joe thought of as his 'interested' face.

'We just thought "Three Little Maids from School" was a good comedy song,' answered Deirdre, 'and that if Tim put new words to it, it might go down well at the concert.'

They were rehearsing in the sunlit parlour of Joe's house, and Dad had popped in before leaving for his evening choir practice at St Peter's church. Joe knew that his father was just being polite, and that the only music he had time for was choral and classical music. The previous week W.S. Gilbert, who wrote the lyrics for the hugely popular Gilbert and Sullivan operettas, had died, and Joe had been taken aback when Dad had dismissed his work as trivial. Joe had argued that his lyrics were really clever, but his father had firmly said they would have to agree to differ. Perhaps

Dad was making up for being discouraging by taking an interest now.

'I'm sure your piece will be very well received,' he said.

'Thanks, Mr Martin.'

'And how did you decide who would do what?'

'Well, Deirdre is the best musician,' answered Tim, 'so she'll play the piano, as well as sing.'

'And Tim is the best singer and actor, so he'll take the lead,' added Deirdre,

'And I'm the best footballer – so I'll take a back seat!' said Joe.

'No, your harmonies really add to it,' said Deirdre.

'As long as I can stay in tune.'

'Of course you will. But we've lots of polishing to do between now and Sunday.'

'Well, practice makes perfect, as my choir master likes to say,' intoned Dad.

Joe knew his father meant well but he wished he didn't sound so stiff. Whenever the three friends were in Kavanaghs, Mr Kavanagh seemed relaxed and natural, and Joe couldn't help wishing that Dad was more like him. No sooner had he entertained the thought than he felt guilty of disloyalty.

'Anyway, I'd better leave you to it,' said his father, nodding in farewell, then making for the parlour door.

'Bye, Mr Martin,' said Tim.

'Bye, Dad.'

Deirdre smiled and nodded, playing the opening bars of 'Three Little Maids From School Are We' on the piano as Mr Martin exited.

'You can stop now,' said Joe when he heard the front door closing.

'OK' said Tim, 'let's plan this break-in.'

Deirdre rose from the piano stool and the three friends sat in a circle.

'I cycled over to Iona Road this morning,' said Tim, 'when you were at the dentist, Joe, and Deirdre was in town with Ma. The good news is that Wilson's house has a lane behind it, and the back wall isn't too high.'

'Great,' said Joe.

'I also saw the housekeeper leave the house with a shopping basket to get the messages. And we know from the newspapers that Mr Wilson isn't married. So what would Sherlock Holmes deduce from that?' asked Tim.

Joe considered for a moment. 'Eh...Wilson has no wife and children. And the houses on Iona Road are nice and solid, but not huge. And he's a member of the Kildare Street Club, where he probably eats some of the time. So, I'd say he probably just employs a housekeeper. And she might not be full time.'

'Good thinking, Watson!' said Tim.

Joe grinned. 'So, hopefully there won't be any other servants in the house.'

'If the housekeeper goes for the messages around the same time tomorrow morning that would be the time to strike,' suggested Deirdre.

'We've no guarantee she'd go at the same time each day,' said Joe.

'Nothing is guaranteed,' conceded Deirdre. 'But it's likely that she has a routine.'

'And she was gone for about twenty-five minutes today,' said Tim. 'So that's the maximum we should allow ourselves in the house tomorrow.'

'Less,' said Deirdre. 'Allow five minutes at either end for getting in and getting out. Say fifteen minutes in the house.'

'Well, the first thing is to check the garden,' said Joe. 'For any signs of something being recently buried.'

'OK,' said Tim. 'Though I doubt that he's buried the painting in his own garden.'

'Still, it won't take long to check, so we should do it,' said Joe.

'Inside the house, though,' said Deirdre, 'what do we concentrate on?'

'Well, finding the painting would be ideal,' answered Tim. 'Failing that, we look for letters, diaries, address books, appointments. Anything that links Mr Wilson with someone who could buy a stolen painting, or transport it, or store it.'

'Right,' said Joe.

'About the break-in itself, I've had a couple of ideas,' said Deirdre. 'First of all, do you still have the football whistle?'

'Yes,' answered Joe. 'Why?'

'I thought that whoever is keeping watch outside could blow the whistle if the housekeeper is returning. To warn the person inside.'

'That's not a bad idea,' said Tim.

Joe nodded. 'Yes, that makes sense. The housekeeper would have no idea what the whistle was being blown for. The other thing you said though – about the person inside. Are you suggesting that just one of us goes in?'

'Yes,' said Deirdre. 'One person hanging around on the street by themselves for twenty-five minutes stands out more. But two can be chatting or playing a game. It would look more natural.'

'There is that,' said Joe. 'So, which of us searches the house?'

'I'll take that on,' said Tim.

'No,' said Deirdre, 'I'll do it. That would work better.'

Joe was surprised but before he could reply Deirdre continued.

'You didn't think the person breaking in would be a girl, did you?'

'Well… no, not really.'

'That's exactly why I should do it. People don't think of twelve-year-old girls as burglars. They're much more likely to think that boys are up to mischief in a back lane. And you and Tim can play marbles together out on the road while keeping watch. Lots of times you'll see two boys doing that, so it won't look suspicious.'

Joe's instinct was to protest, but he knew that what Deirdre had said was true.

'You'd have to get over the back wall, Deirdre,' said Tim.

'You said yourself that it's not that high. And you or Joe can give me a bunk up. Come on, Tim, you know I'm a better climber than you.'

'It's just—'

'Just nothing! It makes sense. And I'm smaller than Joe, so it will be easier for me to get in through a downstairs window.'

'I don't know,' said Tim.

'You're just saying that because I'm a girl and you're my brother!' Deirdre turned to face Joe and looked him in the eye. 'You know this make sense, Joe. Doesn't it?'

Joe hesitated. But Deirdre's gaze was unflinching, and eventually he found himself nodding.

'Yes,' he said. 'I suppose it does.'

'That's settled then,' said Deirdre. 'We go tomorrow morning, and I search the house.'

CHAPTER SIX

Another bright day had dawned with a clear blue sky, and there was a fresh, summery smell in the air. Maura and Beth Breslin had chalked out a piggy bed on the pavement outside the park at the centre of Great Western Square, and the girls were playing the street game known as beds. This involved hopping and landing on numbered squares, while an empty polish tin filled with clay acted as the piggy that had to be thrown, then pushed by foot, before hopping on the squares.

'Your go, Deirdre,' said Maura, handing her the piggy.

'Thanks,' said Deirdre, taking her place and preparing to throw the piggy and hop. She was planning to head off for Iona Road at 9.30 with Tim and Joe, but in the meantime she was glad of the distraction that playing beds provided.

Yesterday she had felt excited when the boys had agreed to let her be the one to search Mr Wilson's house, but when she woke this morning the enormity of what they were planning hit her. If she got caught inside the house she would be arrested like a common criminal. It was a terrifying thought, and she had tried to push it to the back of her mind.

After breakfast she had seen her father carefully polishing his shoes for his appointment with the authorities. Something about his need to look his best had moved her, and she had felt a surge of affection for him that made her determined to do anything that was necessary to clear his name.

Now, though she tried to lose herself in the game of beds, and she accurately threw the piggy, then slightly hoisted her skirt and hopped lightly onto the appropriate squares. Deirdre completed a circuit, then looked up and saw that Sadie Nolan had just arrived. Sadie's family lived in a somewhat bigger house than Deirdre's on the east side of Great Western Square. Unlike Joe, whose house was also larger, Sadie liked to lord it over other people, which Deirdre hated.

"Morning, girls,' she said now.

'Hello, Sadie,' answered Maura and Beth.

'Sadie,' said Deirdre in greeting.

'Deirdre. Didn't think I'd see you this morning.'

'Why not?'

'I heard your father and the other suspects are being questioned again. I think if it was me I'd be in the church praying it went well.'

'My father isn't a *suspect*!' said Deirdre.

'I don't think that's how the police see it.'

'Really?'

'Yes, really. He was the guard on the train, Deirdre. And the painting was stolen when he should have been guarding it.'

'He had nothing to do with that.'

'Let's hope you're right,' said Sadie with mock sincerity. 'It would be awful to have to visit him in jail.'

Deirdre felt something snap inside her. The last time she had clashed with Sadie Nolan she had held back, knowing Mr Nolan was senior to Da in work. But this time Deirdre didn't care about any of that. 'You know what, Sadie,' she said. 'You're useless at sport – but take a running jump at yourself anyway!' She threw the piggy down at the feet of the other girl, who jumped aside nervously, then Deirdre turned abruptly and walked away.

* * *

'Gotcha!' cried Tim. He had skilfully rolled a coloured marble, to knock one of Joe's marbles out of the way as they played on the pavement on Iona Road. From where they were situated, Tim could keep an eye on Mr Wilson's house, while still being far enough away not to be obvious to anyone who might look out its front window.

Joe handed over the marble that Tim had won, then glanced towards the house. 'Still no sign of the housekeeper,' he said.

Tim nodded. 'It's like Ma says. 'A watched kettle never boils.''

A horse-drawn breadman's cart in the livery of Johnson, Mooney and O'Brien came clip-clopping down the road, and Tim saw the breadman rein to a halt, then deliver loaves to several of the houses. He didn't call to the Wilson home, however, and Tim was glad, figuring that it increased the chances of the housekeeper stepping out to buy bread and other groceries.

It was now a little later than the time yesterday when the housekeeper had emerged, but Tim forced himself to remain patient. He had the football whistle in his pocket, he and Joe were in position, and Deirdre was ready to go into action as soon as the coast was clear.

'OK,' said Joe, 'let's set up for another game.'

'All right.'

'And let's hope this housekeeper goes out soon.'

'Amen to that,' said Tim. 'Amen to that.'

* * *

The scent of incense and candle wax lingered in the air, and Deirdre breathed in deeply, savouring the aroma. It was a unique smell she only encountered in churches, and combined with the cool interior of St Columba's church, it made for a calming, peaceful atmosphere. She had slipped on a beret to cover her head, as was expected of girls in a place of worship. She reasoned that it made sense to wait in the church rather than in the lane behind the house while awaiting word from the boys. The church was only yards from the house, and as soon as she got the signal she would be ready to act.

Deirdre wasn't normally given to nerves, but now that they were carrying out the plan she was more on edge than she had expected. One of the things she hadn't fully thought through was the effect on Da if she got caught breaking and entering. She was doing it, of course, to try to help prove his innocence. But if she got arrested for burglary it would make things look even worse for Da.

Reaching into her pocket, she took out a coin. She crossed to the nearest shrine, dropped the coin in the slot, and took up a white wax candle. She lit the candle from one that was already burning, then placed it in a line of other candles that flickered in front of a statue of the Virgin Mary. Deirdre knelt down and blessed herself. Then she prayed hard that all would go well.

* * *

'Look, Joe!' cried Tim. 'She's leaving!'

Tim watched with excitement as a middle-aged woman stepped out the front door of the Wilson house. She was the same woman that he had seen yesterday, and today she also carried a wicker shopping basket as she set off down the road.

'Thank God for that,' said Joe.

'Yeah, I was starting to think she'd never go out.'

'OK, we know the plan,' said Joe, scooping up the marbles, 'let's do it!'

Both boys crossed the road, and Tim watched as his friend continued on until he got to the gate of the church. He saw Joe stopping outside the church, ready to notify Deirdre once it was safe. But first Tim knew he had to establish that there was no-one else in Wilson's house.

He opened the garden gate and stepped up to the front door. He gathered himself, then knocked firmly. He fervently hoped that there would be no answer, but if there was he was going to ask if this was the Kelly household, and pretend that he had the wrong house number.

He found himself holding his breath, then his spirits began to rise when he got no answer. Just to be sure, he knocked again. Still he heard nothing. He quickly stepped away from the door and walked back out to the pavement. Then he looked down the road and nodded to Joe, who immediately headed into the church to alert Deirdre.

Tim turned around and walked away, trying to look as casual as possible. But his heart was pounding as they finally got to start their mission.

* * *

Deirdre dropped lightly from the top of the wall down into the garden. She quickly regained her balance, then looked around. She was pleased to see that Mr Wilson's garden had plenty of trees and shrubbery. It meant she wasn't overlooked by neighbours, and she had also managed to climb the wall – aided by the boys – without being observed.

Her plan for entering the house depended on the hot June weather, and she was hugely relieved now to see that a downstairs window was open, probably to cool the kitchen. First, though, she needed to examine the back garden for any signs of recent digging. Like Joe, she didn't believe that Mr Wilson would bury a stolen painting here at home, but it had to be checked all the same.

Starting at the rear wall, she worked her way carefully up the garden. She checked the flower beds, the border alongside the bushes, and a small vegetable patch. She looked intently, seeking any hints of disturbance or a site that had been camouflaged, but she found no sign of anything suspicious. Satisfied with her search, she crossed to the open window and stopped. *This was the point of no return.* Up until now, if challenged, she was going to claim that she was looking for a ball that had been knocked over the wall. But once she went in the window there could be no excuses – she was breaking into a private home, pure and simple. She paused briefly, then she placed her hands on the windowsill, hauled herself up, and climbed feet-first through the open window.

* * *

Joe smelled the stink from the slop cart the moment it turned the corner. The driver, a red-faced man in stained, ragged clothes, guided his tired-looking horse in to the kerb at Iona Road. 'Slops!' he roared in a gravelly voice. 'Slops!'

Joe was glad of the distraction, and he took a break from playing marbles with Tim. He watched as women emerged from several nearby houses carrying buckets of waste food. The sour, decaying smell from the slop cart was made worse by the heat, but Joe knew that the slopman performed a useful function, with the discarded food being used to feed pigs.

Joe had begun to feel conspicuous, despite pretending to be engrossed in the games of marbles with Tim. He remembered the uncomfortable sense of all eyes being on him when he had stepped up to take a vital free kick in the semi-final of the inter-school cup while playing Gaelic football for his school. That moment had passed quickly though, whereas loitering on the pavement had left him feeling in the public eye. Now, however, he reckoned that anybody looking out a window, or passing along the street, would be more likely to look at the activity around the slops being loaded onto the cart, rather than at two boys quietly playing.

'I wonder how Deirdre's doing?' he said.

'If there's anything to find, Deirdre will find it,' said Tim.

'Yeah. It just feels like we've been here for ages.'

'I know. But it's actually only been a few minutes.'

'I suppose.'

'Look on the bright side, Joe. Even if it's awkward for us, the longer the housekeeper is gone, the more time Deirdre has to search.'

'You're right. Sorry, I'm…I'm just being nervy.'

'I'm nervous too, so there's a pair of us in it,' said Tim with a wry grin.

Joe felt a little better and he admired his friend for being honest enough to admit to his own nervousness.

'Right,' said Tim, 'another game of marbles?'

'OK,' said Joe. 'Another game.'

* * *

Deirdre had lost track of time. All her attention was focussed on the task in hand as she examined the contents of Wilson's study. A letter that she had found on his desk was on headed paper from a club called Rules, and was a politely worded request to Mr Wilson, as a gentleman and a club member, to clear a debt of five hundred pounds. The logo on top of the headed paper showed a deck of cards and a roulette wheel, and Deirdre realised that Rules must be a gambling club. *Could Wilson have stolen the painting to pay off gambling debts?* It surely had to be a possibility. But owing a large sum of money wasn't evidence of having committed a crime, and Deirdre knew she had to find something more substantial.

She opened the top drawer of Wilson's desk and took out an

address book. She scanned through it, but nothing about the enclosed names and addresses seemed untoward.

Deirdre replaced the address book exactly where she had found it, then took up another, smaller book. This was a yearly planner, and she examined the current month of June. It was full of appointments, one of which struck her as interesting. It read *Con Furlong, Bailey Maid, Howth Harbour, 11.00 am. Sat 10th June.*

Deirdre's mind began to race. The *Bailey Maid* sounded like a boat. *Why would an art gallery director want to meet someone with a boat in Howth?* Maybe if he wanted to transport something out of the country? Up to now Deirdre had feared that perhaps they were deluding themselves about Mr Wilson being the thief. Now though, it seemed that he owed money and was meeting someone with the means to transport something out of the country. It still wasn't proof. But Deirdre had a gut feeling that they had found their man.

* * *

The boys were lining up the marbles on the pavement for another game when Tim felt Joe grasping his arm.

'Tim!' he cried softly.

'Yes, I see her!' The housekeeper was returning, but she was moving briskly now, in contrast to her more leisurely pace when she had left the house.

'The whistle, Tim!' said Joe, as he scooped up the marbles.

'I know, I know!'

Tim felt his pulses racing. He reached into his pocket and took out the whistle. His mouth was dry, but he quickly inserted the whistle between his lips. He turned his back so that the approaching housekeeper wouldn't see that he was the one blowing it, then blew three shrill blasts.

'We need to distract her!' said Joe.

'What?'

'She's moving too fast. We need to buy time for Deirdre!'

Tim silently cursed the woman for moving so swiftly. Maybe she had dawdled too long at the shops, or maybe she had bought milk that she wanted to get in out of the hot sun. Not that it mattered, she was crossing Iona Road at a smart pace.

'Distract her, Tim!' said Joe.

'How?!'

'I don't know. You're the actor – make up something!'

Tim saw the woman approaching the garden gate. Moving on instinct, he started across the road to intercept her.

'Excuse me!' he said.

'Yes?' said the housekeeper, turning to face him as she opened the gate.

Tim hadn't had time to come up with a plan, and for a second his mind was blank. 'I wonder…could you tell me the time, please?' he asked.

'It's about a quarter to eleven.'

'Thank you. And do you know…do you know what time Mass is in St Columba's?' he continued, desperately improvising.

'It's at eleven,' answered the housekeeper.

'Do you know…which priest is saying the mass?' It felt like a daft question as soon as Tim asked it, but it was the best he could come up with, and every second might count in buying time for Deirdre.

'I haven't a clue,' said the housekeeper with a touch of impatience. She turned away, closed the gate after her, and took out a key for the front door.

'Thank you very much,' said Tim, trying to delay her for even a few more seconds. 'I'll say a prayer for you.'

'Do that,' said the woman brusquely. She turned the key in the lock, stepped inside, and closed the door after her.

Tim hesitated, hoping he had done enough to save Deirdre. Then he turned away and walked towards the lane at the back of the house.

* * *

Deirdre heard the housekeeper leaving the kitchen and starting to ascend the stairs. She felt her knees trembling, but she tried not to panic. *You have the advantage,* she told herself. *The housekeeper has no idea you're here.* Moving quickly, Deirdre crossed the study, dropped to the carpet and crawled under the desk.

She heard footsteps as the woman came up the stairs, and she prayed that the housekeeper was heading for the bathroom or one of the bedrooms. The footsteps continued along the landing, then paused outside the closed-over door of the study. Deirdre found herself holding her breath and hoping the woman wouldn't come in.

After what seemed an eternity but was probably just a second or two, Deirdre heard the creak of the door swinging open. Then the housekeeper stepped into the room.

Deirdre stayed stock still under the desk and tried to keep her breathing absolutely silent. Her heart was pounding, but she knew that she wasn't visible from here. *But if the woman came around the desk...*

The footsteps drew nearer, and Deirdre heard something being placed down on the desk above her head, though the housekeeper was still out of sight. All it would take, however, was for her to round the desk to open a drawer, or to put something in the waste-paper basket, and Deirdre would be visible. And not just visible, but trapped with no way of escape.

She waited in an agony of suspense, then she heard footsteps again and the creak of the door. Her instinct was to breath a huge sigh of relief, but she stopped herself. Supposing the housekeeper had spotted her and was playing cat and mouse, and waiting out on the landing to catch her out? No, that wasn't realistic, she told herself. The woman had come in to place a package or a letter on Mr Wilson's desk. If she had seen Deirdre's foot sticking out behind the desk she would have reacted at once. But although Deirdre had evaded detection for now she still had to find a way to get out of the house unseen.

She crawled silently out from her hiding place and got to her feet. From out on the landing she heard a door being shut, and she crossed to the closed-over door of the study. Opening it gently to minimise the creaking, she peeked out. The door that was closed, and behind which she presumed the housekeeper had gone, was of the toilet on the return landing. With the housekeeper visiting the toilet, this was Deirdre's chance to escape. Then again if she started down the stairs and the woman came out she would be caught red-handed.

She hesitated, then decided that she had to take a chance. With the toilet door closed she reckoned that the creaking of the study door wouldn't be heard. Moving swiftly, she opened the door, and started along the landing. Her heart was pounding madly in her chest. And just as she reached the return landing, she heard the sound of a toilet being flushed. Deirdre started rapidly down the stairs, hoping that the housekeeper would take a few seconds to wash her hands, but aware that she'd be spotted if the woman came out quickly.

Deirdre reached the end of the stairs, dreading to hear the woman's cry of alarm. Instead she reached the front door and got it open. She quickly stepped outside and swung the door behind her, but without making the noise of fully closing it. She walked down the short path and out the gate, ready at any moment to run if she heard a shout. She reached the corner and turned it, taking her out of sight of the Wilson house. Then she paused, breathed out deeply, and walked on to rendezvous with the boys.

CHAPTER SEVEN

'**I** have a cricket joke, Joseph.'

'Yes?' said Joe, unable to keep the surprise from his voice. His father wasn't normally given to telling jokes, and Joe looked at him across the dinner table with interest.

'What's the difference between Cinderella and a batsman who keeps nicking off at the ball?'

'What's the difference?' asked Joe.

'Cinderella knew when to leave the ball!'

Joe laughed, partly at the joke, and partly to encourage his father. It wasn't often that Dad was genuinely light-hearted, and Joe reasoned that it must be the combination of the sunny weather and the prospect of Dad's Saturday afternoon cricket match tomorrow that had him in good form.

Joe too was in good spirits. He felt pleased with the successful break-in earlier in the day at Wilson's house, and he was excited at the plans for tomorrow, when he would meet up with Tim and Deirdre to continue their mission. He was reluctant to alter the relaxed mood with Dad, but all through dinner he had been waiting for the right moment to question him discreetly, and now he felt the time was right.

'Can I ask you a question, Dad?' he said.

'Of course.'

'I just wondered if you heard anything. I know Mr Kavanagh

was to be interviewed today by the police.' As soon as he asked the question Joe sensed the change in the atmosphere, and he almost wished he had kept quiet. But Tim and Deirdre were his friends, and if Dad had any news on Mr Kavanagh's situation Joe wanted to hear it.

'I work for the Midland Great Western Railway, Joseph. I'm not part of the police investigation.'

'But you're a senior clerk, Dad. People in Head Office must have been talking.'

'Well, of course some people will gossip – or even rumour-monger. I make a point of avoiding that.'

'Did you not hear anything at all? It's just, I'm really worried, Dad, for Tim and Deirdre.' Joe knew that he was taking a risk in pressing his father. Dad had reluctantly allowed him to stay friends with Tim, and it was always possible that he might change his mind. Even so, Joe felt that any inside information could be valuable.

'What I did hear was the value of the stolen painting,' said Dad.

'And?'

'It's worth a fortune. Thousands of pounds.'

'Gosh. And today's interviews? Did they shed any light…or is there–'

'There's nothing,' his father said, cutting him off. 'No new evidence.'

'That's not good news for Mr Kavanagh.'

'No, Joseph, it's not.'

'I'm dead sure he's innocent, Dad.' When his father didn't respond, Joe looked him in the eye. 'Do you still believe that too?'

Dad hesitated, then slowly nodded. 'Yes, actually, I do. But the fact is the Midland Great Western Railway agreed to transport a valuable painting, and it was stolen. And stolen on Mr Kavanagh's watch.'

Joe wanted to say that it could have been stolen before that, but he knew that his father was conservative. Dad would regard the idea of a director of the National Gallery stealing a painting as outlandish.

'So, what do you think will happen next, Dad?'

'The police and the company are under pressure – huge pressure – to solve the case. I imagine they in turn will put pressure on all the suspects, and hope someone cracks. Other than that, I don't see a solution.' Dad raised his hand to ward off further questions. 'Now, enough of doom and gloom.'

'Right.'

'Apple tart for dessert, how does that sound?'

'Good,' said Joe, trying hard for a smile. 'It…it sounds good.'

* * *

'I heard a brilliant story about Howth,' said Tim.

'Oh, what's that?' asked Mam.

Tim was sitting with Deirdre and his parents at the kitchen table, the air pungent with vinegar as they had their Friday treat of fish and chips. He could see that Da was still subdued after his police questioning earlier in the day, and Tim hoped that he might distract him with the story. Deirdre and Tim had arranged with Joe to track Mr Wilson on his journey to Howth tomorrow. They had told their parents that they were going there on a picnic, and so Tim reckoned that it seemed natural enough now to try to engage Da with a story about Howth.

'Well,' said Tim, 'When I say I *heard* the story, that's not exactly true. I actually read it in a library book.'

'Stop making a meal of it and tell us the story!' said Deirdre.

'I'm just about to,' said Tim, quickly sticking his tongue out at his sister, then speaking quickly before he could be reprimanded. 'You've heard of Granuaile, haven't you?' he said.

'Yes,' answered Da, 'in olden times she was the Queen of Connaught.'

'Didn't they call her the Pirate Queen?' asked Ma.

Tim nodded, 'She had a fleet of ships, and she operated out of Galway in the fifteen hundreds.'

'What's that got to do with Howth?' said Deirdrc.

'The story goes that she sailed into Howth and went to call on the St Lawrence family, the Lords of Howth Castle, to have dinner with them.'

'Was the castle there all those years ago?' queried Ma.

'Yes, according to the story. Anyway, she found the gates of the castle closed, so Granuaile was offended, and she took the son of the house, Christopher St Lawrence, hostage, until the family apologised.'

'Maybe a slight over-reaction?' said Ma.

'Maybe,' agreed Tim. 'But it worked. She didn't release him until the family apologised. And do you want to know the really good part?'

'No, tell us the really boring part,' said Deirdre sarcastically.

Tim ignored his sister, pleased instead to see from Da's expression that his curiosity had been sparked.

'What's the really good part?' asked his father.

'For over three hundred years the St Lawrence family kept the castle gates open at dinner time, and they set an extra place at their dinner table for unexpected guests.'

'Seriously?' asked Mam.

'Yes,' said Tim. 'And according to my library book they still do it to this very day.'

'That's crazy,' said Deirdre.

'But true.'

'Well, be the hokey, but you learn something new every day,' said Da.

This was the liveliest Tim had seen Da all day, and he was pleased that the story had gained his interest. Mam caught Tim's eye, and gave a tiny nod, as if to say well done.

'Good story, Tim,' said Da. 'And now I have…I have something to say.'

His father paused, and Tim had no idea what was coming.

'I know this last while has been hard, and I haven't been in the best of form,' said Da. 'But I just want to say ye've all been great, standing four square behind me and looking out for me.'

His father looked Tim in the eye, and it struck Tim that maybe Da was smarter than he had thought, and that he knew that Tim had been trying to distract him.

Da stood slowly and opened his arms. 'Come here to me, both of you.'

Tim and Deirdre rose from opposite sides of the table and stepped into his arms. Da hugged them both tightly.

'You're the best any father could have,' he said. 'The very best.'

Tim felt a lump in throat, and he swallowed hard then looked up at this father. 'So are you, Da,' he said softly. 'So are you.'

* * *

The wheels of an out-of-control horse and cart skidded on the cobblestones as it came careening around the corner, heading straight for Joe. He could see the wild-eyed look in the horse's eyes and the panicked look on the driver's face as he hauled on the reins, trying in vain to halt the bolting animal. The roadway was shrouded in fog and only partly illuminated by the street gas lamps, making the sudden appearance of the galloping horse all the more dramatic.

Normally Joe liked fog and the magical way it made an ordinary landscape seem mysterious. In fact, he liked the way Great Western Square looked in all the different seasons, from balmy summer nights when the starry sky was a deep blue, to frosty autumn evenings with a bite in the air, to his favourite, the depths of winter with the square covered in a blanket of snow. Tonight though, the fog seemed more creepy than magical, and Joe stood rooted to the spot as the runaway horse burst out of the fog and made straight for him.

He tried to scream, but as so often happened with nightmares, he couldn't make a sound, then just as he seemed about to be run over, he woke with a start. His heart was pounding, and beads of perspiration had formed on his forehead. He made a conscious effort to breathe deeply, relieved that he had woken from the nightmare, yet disturbed that he had had the dream again.

He had a recurring dream a couple of times every year, and each time he stood helpless as the bolting horse thundered terrifyingly towards him. Nothing like that had ever happened him in real life, yet dreaming that he couldn't move to escape a galloping horse was always the core of the dream. Before his mother had died, he would go to her after his nightmares, and she always managed to soothe him and get him back to sleep. But he was twelve years old now and he didn't feel he could wake Dad just because he had had a bad dream.

He sensed that the dream was about loss of control, and he wondered what had brought it on.

Lying in the dark, he reviewed what could be affecting him. A possible worry was Sunday's concert for the residents. There was always the risk that his comedy song with Tim and Deirdre would fall flat on its face. But even if it wasn't well received, that would soon be forgotten, considering everything else that was going on right now. And that, he realised, was much more likely the cause of his dream. Although it felt exciting to be on a mission to investigate Mr Wilson, there was still a question mark over Mr Kavanagh's future with the Midland Great Western Railway. And if they failed in their mission to prove him innocent, things could spiral out of control, with Mr Kavanagh losing his job and Tim and Deirdre losing their home.

Joe still felt shaken by the nightmare, but now that he had figured out what had probably brought on the dream, he felt a little better. And maybe tomorrow in Howth they would get some answers about what Mr Wilson was up to. Meanwhile he needed his rest. He mopped his brow, turned over on his side, and lay still in his darkened bedroom, hoping that sleep would come.

CHAPTER EIGHT

'Are you all set for tomorrow night's concert?'

Deirdre thought for a moment before answering. Bright early morning sunlight flooded in through the window of the local shop where she was buying supplies for the picnic in Howth, and Deirdre shielded her eyes as she answered Mrs Garvey, the shopkeeper.

'You're never all set,' she said lightly. 'You always feel you could do with more rehearsal.'

'I don't know how you do it at all,' said Mrs Garvey. 'I'd sooner die then get up in front of a crowd of people.' Mrs Garvey was a stout, middle-aged woman who ran the shop with her husband, and Deirdre liked her.

'I love music, but to be honest, Mrs G, it is a bit scary when the moment comes,' admitted Deirdre. 'That's probably why we always feel we could rehearse more. Even though we *are* prepared, and there's a point when you have to just stop and say: "That's it".'

'And that's where you are now?' said Mrs Garvey.

'No, actually we're having another rehearsal tomorrow morning.'

'I thought there's a point when you have to stop?'

'There is. But I also said you're *never* all set!' answered Deirdre with a laugh.

Mrs Garvey smiled good-naturedly, and Deirdre took up the

brown paper bag containing her purchases.

'Oh, one last thing. An ounce of tobacco for your da,' said the shopkeeper, sliding the packet of tobacco across the counter.

'But Da didn't ask me to buy tobacco.'

'I know. There's no charge, it's on the house.'

Deirdre was taken aback, and Mrs Garvey reached out and squeezed her arm.

'Just a little goodwill gesture, Love. Your da is a fine, decent man, and it's not right the way he's been treated.'

'Thank you…thank you so much.'

'No need for thanks, pet. Tell him to just enjoy a few pipes of tobacco.'

'I will, Mrs Garvey.'

'And enjoy your day trip to Howth – don't fall into the harbour!'

'I'll try not to,' said Deirdre, then she waved in farewell and made for the door. She stepped happily out into the June morning, encountering Sadie Nolan who was about to enter the shop.

'Sadie,' she said in muted greeting.

'Pushing your concert, were you?' said Sadie, indicating a poster for the show in the shop window.

'No, I don't think we need to push it.'

'Cocky, aren't you?'

'No.'

'Yeah, you are. Just cause you can play the piano you think you're great.'

'Not great.' *But better than you, though that's not saying much.* It was what Deirdre wanted to say, but she stopped herself. She didn't want to add to Da's difficulties by alienating the family of anyone who might have standing in the Midland Great Western Railway. Deirdre took a breath, then spoke calmly. 'I'm just happy to play in a concert that everyone can enjoy. Happy is good, Sadie. You should try it.'

Deirdre could see that Sadie was unsure how to respond, and before she could say anything, Deirdre turned away and walked off down the sunlit street.

* * *

Thick, black smoke belched from the engine, and the train slowed down as it approached Amiens Street station. Tim sat with Joe and Deirdre in the last carriage of the train. They had discreetly followed Mr Wilson from his home in Iona Road to Drumcondra train station, then made sure to sit in a different carriage to their quarry. From Mr Kavanagh's description they had recognised him at once when he emerged from his house – a dapper, well-tailored man in his forties who carried himself with the assured bearing of a gentleman. Tim had reasoned that if Wilson had to travel to Howth for a noonday meeting – which they knew from Deirdre reading his appointments diary – then he would have to get off this train in Amiens Street and take a connecting train to the terminus in Howth. It meant that the three friends could stay out of his sight in another carriage and still be sure of not losing him.

'This is like the way Sherlock Holmes and Watson went by train in their adventures,' said Joe, happily sitting back in his seat.

'Except they travelled first class,' answered Tim.

'True,' said Joe. 'But let's see how well up you are. What London stations did they travel from?'

'Ah, lads,' said Deirdre.

'Waterloo, Liverpool Street, Paddington in the *Boscombe Valley Mystery*,' replied Tim.

'Please, boys. Enough of the Sherlock Holmes stuff.'

'I don't know how you can't see that they're brilliant stories,' said Tim.

'We've had this before,' answered Deirdre. 'You and Joe love them, I don't. Can the three of us go to Howth without Holmes and Watson tagging along?'

'All right,' said her brother raising his hands in surrender. 'But you're the one missing out,' he added.

'You always have to have the last word, don't you?'

'No.'

'That's an example of it, right there.'

'You asked me a question!' protested Tim.

'OK,' said Joe, raising a hand to stop them, 'OK. I've got a surprise that I was going to show you in Howth. But to stop the bickering I'll show you now.' He began to undo the straps of his rucksack, and Tim immediately dropped the argument with his sister and watched with interest as Tim removed a pair of binoculars

'Wow!' said Deirdre, 'They look great'

'They're pretty powerful all right,' said Joe. 'Sometimes Dad uses them for bird watching when we're on holidays.'

'And he lent them to you?' asked Tim.

'Eh…you could say that. It's just he doesn't *know* he's lent them to me.'

'Generous of him all the same,' said Deirdre with a grin.

'I'm a dead man if they get damaged, or I lose them.'

'So, what made you bring them?' asked Tim.

'I don't think Mr Wilson has the faintest notion that we're tailing him. But still, we don't want to catch his attention any more than we have to. With the binoculars we can watch what he's doing without needing to go near him.'

'Smart thinking,' said Deirdre.

'Absolutely,' agreed Tim,

'Right,' said Joe. 'When he gets to Howth it'll be interesting. And with these, we can watch him like a hawk.'

'Great,' said Joe, as the engine entered Amiens Street station and came to a halt in a cloud of white steam. Then he rose from his seat, eager to change trains, and to find out what awaited them in Howth.

The salty sea air had a tang to it, and the summer breeze carried a faint scent of fish from the harbour. A brass band was playing 'The Blue Danube' on the seafront, and day-trippers spilled out of the train station, eager to enjoy the summer atmosphere of Howth on a June Saturday.

Joe, Deirdre and Tim had hung well back as Mr Wilson had left the train and made his way towards the west pier. The three friends had stayed at the rear of the crowd exiting the station, and now they sat on a low wall at the harbour. They were eating candy floss that Deirdre had bought them, partly as a treat, and partly to make them fit in with the other day-trippers.

Joe took a mouthful of candy floss, then raised the binoculars to his eyes. He was pretending to scan the harbour and pier casually, though in fact he was following the progress of Mr Wilson.

'What's he doing?' asked Deirdre.

'Walking slowly like he's out for a stroll.'

'How well can you see him with the binoculars?' asked Tim.

'Like he was a few feet away. Don't worry, I'll tell you the minute he meets anyone.'

'OK,' said Deirdre.

'I wonder who invented candy floss?' mused Tim. 'I mean, there's nothing in it, it's like eating sticky air.'

'That's the thanks I get,' said Deirdre.

'I'm just saying–'

'Hang on, folks,' interrupted Joe. He had been holding the binoculars to his eyes with his left hand and eating from the stick of candy floss with his right. Now he gave the stick to Deirdre and used both hands to focus on Wilson.

'What's happening?' asked Deirdre.

'He's stopped at a trawler.'

'Can you see the name of it?' said Tim.

Joe swivelled the binoculars to view the bow of the ship. 'Yes, it's the *Bailey Maid*.' He knew that Tim would be recording this in his notebook, but he didn't turn to look at his friend and instead swung the binoculars back to watch Wilson again.

'Is he going on board?' asked Deirdre.

'No, but he's talking to a man on the deck of the trawler,' answered Joe. 'It looks…it looks like they're arguing.'

'I wonder should we have chanced getting nearer?' she said. 'Then we might have overheard them.'

'No point saying that now,' argued Tim.

'Hang on,' said Joe. He watched as the trawlerman pointed in the direction of Howth Head, whose summit rose to the south of the fishing village. Further words seemed to be exchanged between the two men, then Wilson turned abruptly away. 'He's coming back!' said Joe.

'That was a quick meeting,' said Deirdre.

'I'd say that's not the person he was meant to meet,' suggested Joe. 'The trawlerman pointed up to the Head. I reckon that's where Wilson is headed.'

'Then we don't want him walking by us on his way back,' said Tim. 'Let's mingle with the crowd over at the band.'

'Right,' said Joe, slipping the binoculars back into his rucksack and taking his candy floss back from Deirdre.

They left the harbour wall behind and walked towards the grassy area where the brass band was now playing 'Swanee River'.

'I've been thinking,' said Deirdre as they sat on the grass as though listening to the music. 'If he's going up the Head, he'll probably take the Hill of Howth tram. So, if we're following him, and he's on the upper deck we should stay downstairs. And if he's downstairs, we should take the upper deck.'

'That makes sense,' said Joe. 'And here he comes now.'

They watched as Mr Wilson came back along the pier, moving a little more quickly now. Joe waited until he turned right for the station, which was also the terminus for the tramline, then he looked at the others. 'All right?'

'OK,' said Tim, 'Let's get after him.'

They rose from the grass, and Tim thought that in a Sherlock Holmes story this was where Holmes would say that the game was afoot. Not wanting to annoy Deirdre, Joe resisted saying it. But he sensed that the game *was* afoot, and he felt the thrill of the chase as they started off after their quarry.

* * *

'Look, wild goats!' cried Deirdre, rising from her seat on the open-air upper deck of the Howth tram as it trundled up the gorse-covered slopes of Howth Hill.

'Gosh, look at the horns on that ram!' said Tim.

'I didn't know they lived wild up here,' said Joe.

'Sure look around, it's a perfect place for them,' said Deirdre, indicating the rugged landscape. The heather-bedecked hillside rose steeply before them, while to their rear could be seen the green slopes leading down to the fishing harbour of Howth, with the island of Ireland's Eye rising dramatically from the sparkling waters of the Irish Sea. Holding onto the rail of the tram, Deirdre stayed standing, and looked behind her at the unfolding view. In the distance she could see the golden sands of Portmarnock Beach where Ma and Da sometimes brought her on family outings, and further north on the far horizon she saw the faint outline of the Mourne Mountains.

For a moment she allowed herself to enjoy the spectacular view, then she sat down again aware that she mustn't get distracted. Mr Wilson was in the downstairs compartment of the tram, and she thought again about what he was doing in Howth. The obvious answer seemed to be that he planned to use a fishing boat to smuggle the painting out of the country. But how would he get the painting to Howth? And what was the background of the fisherman? And come to that, how would the director of an art gallery even know the skipper of a trawler?

But then again, he'd hardly have stolen the painting if there wasn't a willing buyer for it. And a buyer involved in art theft might well have the criminal connections that involved transporting contraband by sea. Her thoughts were interrupted as the tram slowed, and the driver called out 'Summit Stop!'

The tram came to a halt, and Deirdre looked over the rail to see if Mr Wilson would get off.

'Any sign of him?' asked Tim.

'Not yet,' said Deirdre. 'No, wait! He's getting off, let's go!'

The three friends rose, then followed the other passengers who were descending the stairs of the tram. Deirdre had convinced the boys that while the binoculars had been useful, now they needed to get closer to Wilson and try to hear what he said to whoever he was meeting. They had agreed that all three of them wouldn't tail him closely at once, but instead would take turns, to lessen the likelihood of being noticed.

Deirdre waited impatiently as the people ahead of her got off the tram, then when it was her turn she alighted quickly. She looked around, unable to see Wilson in the crowd at the busy summit stop. She felt a little panicky and looked in all directions. Suddenly she spotted him, walking in the direction of the Summit Inn. 'OK,' she said relievedly, turning back to the boys.

'Like we agreed. I'll go first while you hang back,'

'Right,' said Tim.

'Good luck,' added Joe.

Deirdre nodded in acknowledgement, then she turned away and walked briskly after Wilson.

* * *

On any other day Tim would have been tempted by the Italian ice-cream seller. The man wore a straw hat and stood behind his ornately decorated ice-cream cart, and a queue of day-trippers had formed, coins in hand as they awaited the portions of ice-cream that he handed out. The idea of a cool, creamy treat on a hot day like today made Tim's mouth water, but he forced himself to concentrate on the business in hand.

Deirdre had been following Mr Wilson closely, maintaining a distance of about five yards behind him. Now, however, she hesitated briefly as Wilson suddenly stepped off the pavement and into the outdoor beer garden of the Summit Inn. It had been agreed that if something like this happened then whoever was tailing their quarry would continue on, rather than take a sudden change of direction. Instead, whoever was next in line would take over and follow Mr Wilson.

Now though, Tim got a bad feeling on seeing Deirdre hesitate. He knew that his twin sister was impulsive, and he hoped that she wouldn't break their agreement in her enthusiasm. He held his breath, then after what seemed like a long time, but was probably only a fraction of a second, she continued on her way.

Tim walked on, keeping his stride relaxed, and he casually bounced a small rubber ball that he and Joe normally used to play handball. Although he appeared to be concentrating on catching the ball each time, in reality he was watching Mr Wilson, who seemed to be scanning the drinkers. Tim stepped into the beer garden. The place was busy, with the tables occupied by groups of young men, families that were out for the day, and a sprinkling of solo drinkers. It was one of these that Wilson seemed to identify, and he came to a halt in front of a man on his own and said a few words. Tim saw the man indicate for Wilson to sit, which the gallery director did.

Tim noted that they made a strange pair. Wilson looked clean and well-groomed, and was expensively dressed in a finely-cut, lightweight suit. The other man was heavily-built, but unkempt, and he looked like he hadn't shaved for several days. Tim knew that he wouldn't be able to hear their conversation unless he got close, and so he dropped the ball that he had been bouncing, deliberately letting it roll so that it went along the ground to the rear of Wilson. Tim excused himself to the people at the nearest table, then dropped to the ground to seek the ball. To Tim's relief, Wilson didn't look around, and Tim listened intently as the gallery director spoke in a low but irritated voice.

'You weren't at the boat,' he said.

'No point hanging round there, the engine's broken down.'

'It's still where we were to meet.'

'We're meeting now, aren't we?'

Tim acted as though he was having difficulty reaching the ball under the table, and he listened as the conversation continued.

'How soon will the engine be fixed?' asked Wilson, his upper-class tone a contrast to the trawlerman's harsher accent.

'Might take few days. I'm hoping to meet a mechanic this afternoon.'

'You're *hoping?*

'Relax, it'll all be fine.'

'We need to talk – in private.'

'And we will. Let me finish me pint, and we'll go to my cottage.'

Tim felt that he couldn't pretend to be looking for the ball any longer, and he retrieved it, still making sure to stay out of Wilson's line of sight as he stood up. He saw the trawlerman raising his glass and draining it in one go, then he turned his back on the two men and walked out of the beer garden. He glanced back to see which way the two men were headed, then turned around the corner and went to Joe.

His friend looked at him eagerly. 'Well?'

'He met the man who was supposed to be at the boat,' said Tim. 'The engine is broken, so your man came up here to drink.

They're going now to talk in private in the trawlerman's cottage.'

'Right,' said Joe excitedly. 'Definitely sounds like they're using a fishing boat to get the painting out of the country.'

'Yes. We need to follow them and see where this fisherman lives. They've headed up towards the cliffs.'

'OK, my turn to do the tailing. I'll get after them.'

'And Joe?'

'Yeah?'

'The trawlerman looks pretty tough. Be careful.'

'I will,' said Joe, giving him a thumbs-up sign.

Tim gave him a thumbs-up in return, then watched as his friend set off after the two men.

* * *

The gulls squealed noisily as Deirdre and Tim walked along the cliff path, the blue sea crashing against the shoreline far below them. To their rear the Bailey Lighthouse appeared to stand guard at the outer curve of Dublin Bay, and to the south could be seen the purple outline of the Dublin Mountains. Because of the dramatic scenery the cliff walk was popular, and with plenty of other day trippers about the twins weren't too conspicuous. Even so, Deirdre and Tim made sure to keep well back while following Joe and the two men.

'I can't help feeling kind of guilty,' said Deirdre

Tim looked at her in surprise. 'How do you mean?'

'If the trawlerman looks so tough, and he catches Joe following him...'

'He won't,' said Tim. 'Joe is smart.'

'It's still a risk. And we've brought him into this to help our father, but it's not really Joe's fight.'

'Well...it sort of is,' said Tim.

'How is it?'

'Joe is my friend. My best friend. If his father was in trouble I'd want to help. And I'd take risks if I had to. I'm sure Joe feels the same.'

'Maybe. But...'

'What?'

'It's bad enough that Da might lose his job,' said Deirdre reluctantly. 'But if Joe gets into trouble Mr Martin could be affected too. Supposing he got sacked?'

'He won't be. It's not the same – no-one suspects Mr Martin of stealing the painting.'

'Even so,' said Deirdre, wanting to believe Tim's argument, but still feeling uncomfortable. 'From now on if there's something risky to be done, one of us should do it, not Joe.'

Tim looked thoughtful, then nodded. 'Fair enough. But for now, Joe is the one at the front. So let's just be ready to back him if he needs it.'

'Definitely,' said Deirdre. Then she continued along the sunlit trail, hoping that their friend would be all right.

* * *

Joe carefully hung back, making sure to keep other walkers between himself and the two men as he followed them along the cliff path. At the far horizon the blue of the Irish Sea merged with the cloudless sky, but Joe consciously blocked out the stunning scenery and concentrated on his subjects. They didn't seem to be engaging in much conversation as they walked side by side along the path, but Joe still wished that he could have used the binoculars to watch them closely. Instead, he left the binoculars in his rucksack, not wanting to draw attention by being seen studying fellow walkers.

After a while the trawlerman came to a halt at a small gate, behind which there was a short track leading to a cottage. From a distance Joe could see that the cottage itself was surrounded by a low stone wall, with shrubbery on the side facing the coast, presumably to give shelter from winds coming in off the sea. The building was in an isolated spot, and as he drew nearer, Joe could see that it looked a bit ramshackle. Joe slowed down as he neared the gate, anxious to get his timing right and not to look suspicious by hanging around at the entrance. He saw the trawlerman opening the cottage door and ushering Mr Wilson inside.

Joe reached the gate, took a deep breath to steady his nerves, then opened the gate with as much confidence as he could muster. His heart was racing as he walked towards the house, but he reckoned that Wilson and the trawlerman wouldn't be looking back, and that if he acted like he had every right to be here, then those strolling along the cliff walk would presume that this was his home.

Joe approached the boundary wall of the cottage, making sure to tread lightly so as to make no sound. He passed through an open garden gate, then turned left towards the gable end of the cottage. As soon as he was behind the stone wall and out of sight of those on the cliff walk, he dropped to his hunkers. It seemed unlikely that the cottage owner or Mr Wilson would be looking out the window, but nevertheless Joe scurried forward on his hunkers below the level of the window, then rounded the corner to the gable end of the cottage. There were discarded fishing nets and broken lobster pots strewn around the ground beside the house and Joe proceeded cautiously, taking care not to step on anything. He paused at the gable end of the building, reasoning that the kitchen was probably around at the rear, and that a window might well be open on a hot day like today. He had no idea if anyone else lived here, but if the trawlerman had a family then one of them could come out the back door at any time. The thought made his heart thump, but he forced himself to breathe deeply again. What he was doing was risky, but if he was going to help Tim's father then he had to take risks.

Gathering his nerve, Joe stepped around the corner. To his relief there was nobody in the back garden. There was an outhouse that looked like a toilet, and more rusted and broken fishing equipment was scattered here, beside a badly tended vegetable plot, but more importantly a rear window was wide open. Joe could hear voices, and he approached gingerly. He heard the rough tones of the fisherman, then a more educated, authoritative voice that had to be Mr Wilson. Joe drew as near as he dared, flattening himself against the wall beside the window.

'No, thank you. Mr Furlong, I won't have whiskey. What I want is some clarity.'

So the cottage owner was Con Furlong, Joe noted.

'Well, you won't mind if I've a tipple,' said the man, who seemed unfazed by the irritation in Wilson's voice. 'Then I'll give ye whatever clarity I can.'

Joe heard the sound of drink being poured as Wilson spoke.

'Surely your mechanic can look at the engine, decide what's wrong, and tell you how quickly he can fix it?'

Furlong smacked his lips, and Joe heard a glass being put down on a table.

'It's not that simple,' said the fisherman. 'Until he knows exactly what's wrong, he won't know what parts he needs. And he might have the parts, or he might have to get the parts. It all depends.'

'It's rather lackadaisical, Mr Furlong. I'm anxious to do this business, and you should be too, because the sooner you do, the sooner you'll get paid.'

'We all want a few bob, but there's no point leaving port till we're sure she's seaworthy. The last thing I want is to break down and have to get boarded by the coastguard. Don't think you want that either.'

'Obviously not.'

'Then let's not panic. I'll talk to my fella today. Tomorrow is Sunday so he won't be working then. Give us Monday – and maybe Tuesday as well, to be on the safe side. So let's say we definitely sail on Wednesday. Do you want to give us the package on the day, or would you prefer to be rid of it, and I can store it for you?'

Joe felt a surge of triumph. Any doubts they might have had were now banished, and he was certain that Wilson had stolen the painting, and that Furlong was going to transport it out of the country.

'No, I have it in a safe place,' the gallery director said. 'I'll get it to you on Wednesday.'

And that's when we'll catch you red-handed and have you arrested, thought Joe. For a moment he allowed himself to imagine the scene, with the haughty Wilson being taken into custody. It was an exciting image and as he pictured it Joe's concentration slipped. He clenched his fist in silent celebration, but unwittingly moved in doing so and stepped on a broken piece of a lobster pot. To Joe's horror, there was a sharp snap, and he stood stock still, praying that it hadn't been heard from inside the cottage. But even as he hoped against hope, a part of his brain reckoned that if he could overhear the two men, they in turn could hear sounds from outside.

'What the hell,' said Furlong.

Joe felt his stomach tightening into a knot. He *had* been heard. *And now he was going to be discovered.* He stood rooted to the spot but tried to fight his panic. If he ran now Furlong might catch him, and even if he didn't, he would know that he had been overheard and could change plans accordingly. *He couldn't let that happen.*

Joe heard footsteps approaching the back door, and without any further hesitation he reached forward and knocked on the door before it got opened. Joe had just given the last of three loud knocks when the door swung open, and Furlong stepped out, an aggressive look on his unshaven face.

'I'm really sorry,' said Joe, swaying on his feet and deliberately making his voice shaky. 'Could I get some water. The heat…I'm really dizzy,' he said leaning against the doorpost.

He had read in an adventure story about the hero getting sun-stroke, and he hoped that his improvised symptoms would be convincing. From the corner of his eye he could see that Wilson had stayed inside the house, but Joe's more immediate concern was Furlong, as the fisherman looked him in the eye, his expression suspicious.

'How did you end up at the back of my house?'

'I…I felt really lightheaded on the cliff walk. This…this was the nearest house.'

'Most people would come to the front door.' said Furlong.

'I thought…I thought the kitchen would be round the back. Please…can I just have a glass of water. I feel awful!'

Any unsuspicious person would surely provide the water, but Furlong stared hard at him, and Joe knew that everything was still in the balance. He blinked rapidly and held onto the doorpost as if to steady himself. His mind was racing, and he tried to think one step ahead. Supposing the trawlerman didn't believe him? Might he take him prisoner? Hold him captive till the painting was moved? Or more terrifyingly, silence him permanently? He swallowed hard, then looked dazedly at Furlong and made his voice even shakier. 'Please. Just a glass of—'

'All right,' interjected Furlong bad-temperedly. 'Wait here and I'll get it for you.'

Joe thought they were the most welcome words he had ever heard, but he tried not to let his relief show. 'Thank you,' he said weakly. 'Thank you very much.'

PART TWO

EVIDENCE

CHAPTER NINE

The shrill blast of the starter's whistle pierced the air. 'Come on, Tim! Come on, Deirdre!' cried Ma as the three-legged race got under way. The early afternoon sun bathed Great Western Square in a warm glow, and there was a festive atmosphere as the Residents' Day children's sports event took place.

Tim's leg was tied to Deirdre's, and the twins were doing well as they ran in tandem. From the corner of his eye Tim could see Ma waving her arm vigorously in encouragement and he felt a rush of affection for her. He suspected that she was trying to make up for Da's absence. After Sunday Mass Da had apologetically told Tim and Deirdre that he couldn't face mingling with all the neighbours at the Residents' Day. It was the first time that his father had openly admitted how much the suspicion over the art theft was affecting him, and Tim had told him that he understood.

Deirdre had said afterwards that they should try really hard to win a medal to lift Da's spirits. Unlike Deirdre, Tim wasn't normally competitive when it came to sports, but he tried to stay fully focused now as they ran across the grass. It had been a busy twenty-four hours, what with yesterday's trailing of Mr Wilson in Howth, a final rehearsal this morning of their piece for tonight's concert, Sunday Mass, and now the sports section of Residents' Day. It had been agreed by the three friends to set aside their detective work for today – the trawler was out of action anyway – and to concentrate on the concert and the sports.

'Faster, Tim!' cried Deirdre, 'I don't want to lose to Sadie Nolan!'

Tim and Deirdre had been towards the front of the race, but he could see that Sadie and her partner had drawn level with them. Sadie wasn't a natural athlete, but Tim knew from Deirdre that Sadie had spent hours practising the three-legged technique with her partner, Maura Breslin.

Tim thought it was silly to take a three-legged race that seriously. He also thought that Deirdre shouldn't let Sadie get to her, but he didn't say that. Instead, he tried hard to pick up his pace. His sudden spurt, however, knocked them out of rhythm, and Deirdre tried to alter her stride, but ended up losing her balance. The twins came tumbling to the ground, and Tim knew at once that their race was over.

'What did you do that for?' demanded Deirdre.

'You were the one who said to go faster!'

Deirdre irritatedly untied the rope from around their legs, then they dusted themselves off and rose to their feet.

'Uh-uh, look who's coming,' said Tim.

Still with their legs tied together, Sadie Nolan and her partner were trotting towards Tim and Deirdre, having finished the race.

'Don't lose your temper, D, don't give her the satisfaction,' whispered Tim.

'Tough luck, Deirdre,' said Sadie with mock concern as she

drew to a halt. 'Hard lines, Tim.'

'Well, it was only a three-legged race,' he answered.

'Still, a race is a race, isn't it? And we came second. We're delighted.'

'Are you going to spend the rest of the day with your legs tied together to celebrate?' asked Deirdre.

Tim could see that his sister's retort had annoyed Sadie, but after a second she gave a false grin. 'Not the rest of the day, Deirdre. Just till we collect our prize. Come on, Maura, let's go and get it.'

Tim watched them trot away, then he turned to Deirdre. 'All right, sis,' he said. 'I wouldn't normally give a hoot, but we need to beat them in the wheelbarrow race, OK?'

'Count on it,' said Deirdre.

* * *

Joe heard a knock on his bedroom door, then Dad stepped into the room. 'Do you want to use a little of my hair oil, Joseph? Have to look your best for the audience,' he added with a smile.

'Thanks, Dad,' said Joe, taking the bottle of sweet-smelling oil. They were getting ready for the Residents' Day concert that was due to start in half an hour, and Joe was both nervous and excited about his coming performance.

He had enjoyed the sports in the afternoon, and had come first in the egg and spoon race, loudly cheered on by Tim, Deirdre, an enthusiastic Mrs Kavanagh, and more reservedly by Dad. Now though, Joe was feeling the usual mixture of what he thought of as two parts excitement and one part fear.

'All set for your piece?'

Joe had started to rub the oil into his scalp to hold his hair in place, but he turned to his father with a playful grimace. 'As set as we'll ever be.'

'You're all good performers, and you've rehearsed well. There's nothing to worry about.'

If only you knew, thought Joe. Although his father was clearly referring to the concert, Joe couldn't help but think back to yesterday in Howth when he had had plenty to worry about. Things could so easily have gone wrong with Con Furlong, and despite talking his way out of trouble, Joe had felt really shaken afterwards. Deirdre and Tim had congratulated him on being cool under pressure, and on gaining vital information, but later in the day Joe had found it hard to shake off thoughts of what might have happened. He knew it was wrong to judge people solely on appearances, but there was no denying that the trawlerman looked like the kind of person who could easily be violent. And even if Furlong and Wilson had completely believed his sunstroke story – and Furlong had only accepted it reluctantly – there was still the fact that they now knew what he looked like. That could make things tricky in the next part of their mission, but for now

Joe tried to put it from his mind and concentrate on the concert.

'We'll do our best, anyway, Dad,' he said.

'Careful, Joseph,' said his father. 'Whenever I hear someone say "I'll do my best", I feel they're giving themselves a way out. That they're not fully committed to what they're attempting. Don't go onstage thinking: "I'll do my best." Go on thinking: "We're going to do this really well."'

'OK.'

'You'll be fine, son. But…can I give you one tip, from my own experience with the choir?'

'Sure.'

'When you're singing harmonies, your main job is to stay in tune yourself. So don't listen too much to how Tim and Deirdre are singing – concentrate fully on your own part. All right?'

'All right, Dad.'

Joe was touched by how supportive his father was being, even though he knew Dad didn't actually like the Gilbert and Sullivan material that they were going to parody. He reached out and touched his father's hand. 'Thanks for the advice, Dad,' he said. 'I want to do you proud.'

His father looked slightly taken aback, then he squeezed Joe's hand in return. 'You always do me proud,' he said softly. 'Never be in any doubt about that. And now,' he said more briskly, 'we need to get organised. Drop the hair oil back to me when you're ready, then we'll head over early and get good seats for the concert.

How does that sound?'

'Thanks, Dad,' said Joe, 'that sounds great.'

* * *

Deirdre stepped forward on the makeshift stage and looked out at the audience. The afternoon sports events had been attended by lots of her neighbours, but tonight it seemed like almost every resident of Great Western Square had turned out for the concert.

Deirdre had left the sports day in good spirits after winning the wheelbarrow race with Tim and she had been even more pleased when Ma had persuaded Da to attend this evening's concert. Mam had argued that if Da stayed at home it would look like he had reason to feel guilty, and he had eventually agreed to attend.

Deirdre could see them now seated between their elderly next-door neighbour, Mr Lawlor, and Mr and Mrs Garvey from the local shop. As far as Deirdre could make out people weren't shunning Dad or acting like they thought he was a thief, but she suspected that he still felt uncomfortable, and she wished she could lift the burden that he felt.

It occurred to her that for this brief moment she had a captive audience of his work colleagues and neighbours. She would never have them all gathered like this again and she felt an impulse to remind them of what a good, honest man Da was, and how unjust it was to treat him as a thief. *Should she say something?* She knew Da wouldn't want her to, but maybe it still needed saying. Or would that just draw more unwanted attention?

She hesitated, and she saw Tim looking at her questioningly. She opened her mouth to speak, still unsure what she would say. Then her gut instinct kicked in, and she decided this wasn't the time to make a speech praising Da.

'Good evening, ladies and gentlemen,' she said, projecting her voice as loudly as she could. 'For the next item in the concert, the Con Brio Trio would like to give you our version of "Three Little Maids from School Are We". Or as we call it "Three Little Babes Who Drool Are We".'

This got an immediate laugh, and as Deirdre took her place at the piano, she realised that the audience was on her side. Tim and Joe stepped forward, and at a signal from Deirdre they launched into the song while she accompanied them. Now that they were finally in action Deirdre forgot any nervousness and threw herself into her performance. She felt a surge of satisfaction, with the hours of rehearsal paying off and things going without a hitch. The combination of the parody lyrics and Tim's skill as a comedy performer drew loud laughter from the audience.

Deirdre looked down to where Ma and Da were seated, and Ma caught her eye and gave her a thumbs up. Better still, she could see that Da was laughing.

They started on another verse, and there were more bursts of laughter at the parody lyrics and Tim's playfully daft lead vocal. Even Mr Martin seemed to be amused, Deirdre noticed, when she spotted him in the audience. Finally, the song ended, and Deirdre rose from the piano and took a bow with Joe and Tim. The audience applauded warmly and there were even a couple of cries of 'Bravo'.

Deirdre looked down once more to where her parents sat. Ma was all smiles, but Da had a look of pride on his face as he applauded. Deirdre felt a sudden rush of emotion and before she knew what she was doing she raised her hand to halt the applause. Although the audience looked a little confused, people did stop clapping, and acting purely on impulse, Deirdre spoke. 'Thank you for applauding our song. And I'd like…I'd like to dedicate it to my father, Brendan Kavanagh. He's the best father and…and the best man I've ever known. Thank you,' said Deirdre, unable to keep a catch from her voice.

There was a shocked silence, and Deirdre hoped that Da wouldn't be angry with her. Then people began to clap, and the clapping spread through the audience. To Deirdre's amazement it began to grow in intensity. Mr and Mrs Garvey rose to their feet, then others followed suit. The applause grew louder, and as Deirdre watched more and more people stood. Tim and Joe stood dumbstruck on the stage as the standing ovation continued.

Deirdre realised that this was the community's way of showing that they supported Da, and she felt overwhelmed. She tried not to cry but she couldn't help it, and she stood shakily on the front of the stage as the tears rolled down her cheeks, while the entire audience was now on its feet, and loudly applauding her father.

CHAPTER TEN

'**B**utterfingers!'

'*Butterfingers*?' cried Tim, aggrieved. 'He was right on top of me when he shot, I hadn't a chance!' He rose from the grass on the makeshift pitch in Great Western Square where he had been acting as goalkeeper. He *had* actually touched the ball with his fingertips as it went past him, but even a really good goalkeeper would have struggled to stop a shot from such close range.

His accuser was Paul Dillon a tall, self-confident boy from nearby Monck Place, whose father was a sergeant in the Dublin Metropolitan Police. In fairness to Paul, he had never given Tim a hard time about the art theft, despite his family's police background, but he liked to bark orders when the local boys were playing football, and he wasn't slow to shout his criticisms.

Tim wasn't a skilful footballer, and when the teams were being picked this morning he had been chosen last, and put in goal. It had brought him down to earth after the high of last night, when everyone had congratulated him on his performance in the concert, and the neighbours had shown their support for Da. But being good at football or fighting was what counted with some of the local boys, and Tim wasn't a natural at either. Even so Paul Dillon's unfair criticism had irked him, and he was sorry now that he had joined in the game of football.

Their playing pitch was smaller than usual today as the stage from the concert was still in place on the green. It had been erected by a group of the local men on Saturday, but no effort had been made to take it down on Sunday night after the concert. The Catholic Church had a rule that physical work shouldn't be done on a Sunday, and Tim knew that some of his Protestant neighbours were even more strict when it came to refraining from physical work on the Sabbath Day.

Tim, Deirdre, and Joe had taken their own break for one day from their investigations, knowing that the trawler in Howth was out of action for the moment. Nevertheless, they needed to talk through their next move, and they had arranged to discuss it at their usual picnic spot on the banks of the Tolka later this morning.

'Start diving for the next shot as soon as he goes to shoot!' ordered Paul. 'Don't just stand there waiting!' Paul held out his hands impatiently for Tim to throw him the football.

Tim looked at the other boy and his patience snapped. 'I'll tell you what, Paul. I have to go, but seeing as you know so much about it, why don't you play in goal yourself?!'

He threw the ball and was pleased to see a surprised Paul fumble it, then he turned away and walked swiftly towards the exit gate.

* * *

'Mouth-watering rhubarb tart, if I say so myself!' said Ma as she prepared to slice her homemade cake at the kitchen table.

'What happened to "self-praise is no praise"?' asked Deirdre playfully.

'Doesn't apply to my cooking,' answered her mother with a grin. 'Now,' she added, 'a big slice for you, I suppose?'

'Yes, please.'

'And the same for Tim,' said Mam, cutting more of the tart. 'And sure I'll include one for Joe as well.'

'Thanks, mam,' said Deirdre as her mother wrapped the pieces of tart in grease-proof paper.

'Sure a picnic wouldn't be a picnic without a bit of tart.'

'I won't argue with that,' answered Deirdre.

'And summer wouldn't be summer without loads of picnics. You're right to make the most of it.'

Deirdre was pleased to see her mother so happy. Ever since the art theft Ma had tried to be cheerful, and Deirdre admired how she always made the best of things. This was different, though, and it was heartening to see her looking genuinely happy.

'Where are you off to today?' asked Ma.

'Up to the Tolka. It's lovely there.'

'It is. Just be careful if you're swimming.'

'We always are, Ma, don't worry.' Deirdre gave her mother's arm a reassuring squeeze. To her surprise, Ma reached out and hugged her. 'What...what's that for?' asked Deirdre lightly.

Ma's expression had grown serious, however, and she looked Deirdre in the eye. 'I know I said it last night…but I need to say it again. What you said at the concert, and the way people reacted – it meant the world to your da.'

'I'm glad. I…I didn't plan to say it…it just came out.'

'Coming from the heart is what made it so powerful.'

'Thanks, Ma.' Deirdre didn't want her mother to know that one of the things that had prompted her outburst was overhearing Ma and Da talking about the rumours that were flying around. Apparently, people were claiming that the National Gallery was going to sue the Midland Great Western Railway for a fortune, that Broadstone railway station might have to be sold, that the company could even go under. Although the rumours were pretty wild, Deirdre could still tell that it had all been getting to Da, and she was glad that her impassioned outburst had prompted such a positive response.

Mam hugged her again now, then released her. 'You're a great daughter,' she said softly.

'And you're a brilliant mother.'

Ma smiled, and Deirdre smiled back. She meant every word of it, even though she knew that she didn't want the kind of life that Ma and most of the local women lived. She reckoned that most of the girls in her school would be happy when they grew up to have children and be housewives. Deirdre, however, wanted to work in a music shop – maybe even own one someday – but that was a secret that she had shared with no-one. Before she could think about it any further, the kitchen door opened, and her twin brother entered.

'Oh, here's himself,' said Ma, her mood light-hearted again, 'strolling in now that the picnic is made.'

'Rhubarb tart,' said Tim. 'Sure I suppose someone has to eat it!'

'Go on, you scamp!' said Ma, handing over the wrapped slices of tart. 'Enjoy your picnic.'

'Thanks, we will,' said Deirdre, then she and Tim eagerly took up the food and headed off to meet Joe.

* * *

The heat of the June morning heightened the reedy smell of the river, and the sun sparkled on the slow-flowing waters of the Tolka. Joe breathed in deeply, thinking that the sweet aroma of gorse, mixed with the slightly sour scent of the river was for him the smell of summer. Deirdre had won another swimming race that day and the three friends were seated at their favourite spot on the banks of the Tolka. Before tucking into their picnic, Joe knew that decisions had to be made.

'OK, we had a day off, and it was great. But what's next?' he asked.

'I've been thinking about it a lot,' said Deirdre.

'And?'

'Maybe we should just go to the police.'

'I don't think so,' said Tim.

'Why not?'

'For the obvious reason, D. They'll just say you're looking for someone to blame so as to clear Da.'

'Unless...' said Joe, half-thinking out loud.

'Unless what?' said Tim.

'Supposing *I* was the one who went? They couldn't claim I was trying to save a relative.'

'They couldn't,' agreed Tim. 'But your own father would have a fit if you got involved with the police.'

Joe tried to think of an answer, but what Tim had said was true. Joe hated Dad's reaction when he disappointed him – he hadn't even been able to tell Dad that when he grew up he wanted to be an engineer, rather than a clerk like him.

'Besides,' his friend continued, 'we still don't have enough evidence for them to take us seriously.'

'Well, now we know for sure that Mr Wilson is the thief,' said Deirdre. 'And we know how he plans to get the painting out of the country. We didn't know any of that at the start.'

Tim turned to his sister. 'But what do we say to the police? That you broke into somebody's house? And our pal overheard a conversation in Howth? That won't work.'

'So, what *will* work?'

'This might sound a bit mad,' said Joe. 'But maybe...maybe

we could sabotage the engine of the trawler? Then they couldn't move the painting out of the country.'

Deirdre looked dubious. 'How would you even begin to sabotage an engine?'

'I know a bit about machines,' said Joe. 'I…I haven't figured it all out, but–'

'That could wreck the trawler,' cut in Tim. 'That's probably the man's livelihood.'

'Don't be such a goody-two-shoes,' said his sister. '*Crime* is probably his livelihood, and we're trying to solve a crime our father's accused of.'

Tim raised a hand in surrender. 'All right, I was just saying.'

'Let's not bicker,' said Joe. 'The question is, what do we actually do next?'

'I think we have to catch Wilson and Furlong red-handed with the painting,' said Tim.

'That's going to be pretty hard,' said Deirdre. 'We don't know exactly when Wilson will move it.'

Joe considered this. 'We could keep a watch on the cottage.'

'He might go straight to the trawler.'

'We could split up and watch both,' said Deirdre.

Joe had a thought, and he mulled it over briefly before turning to his friends. 'We could do something simpler. You're right, Tim, even if we spoke to the police, they probably wouldn't take a twelve-year-old seriously. But supposing they got an anonymous letter? Telling them that Wilson is crooked, and they should check up on him, and saying about his link with Con Furlong?'

Deirdre nodded approvingly. 'That might get their attention all right.'

Joe turned to his friend. 'Tim?'

Tim looked thoughtful, then spoke. 'Why not? I can't see what we have to lose.'

'OK,' said Joe. 'We'll have to compose the letter very carefully.'

'And maybe do it in capital letters so it's hard to tell if it's adult handwriting or not?' suggested Deirdre.

'Good idea,' said Joe.

'Meanwhile I have a suggestion,' said Tim. 'Supposing we treat this like a chess problem.'

'A chess problem' repeated Deirdre dubiously.

'Yes. We try to think up every move they could make, and then we decide what our counter-move should be. What do you think?'

'I think Sherlock Holmes would be proud of you,' said Joe. 'So yes, let's get started. What's the first move?'

'What has you up so early?' asked Da, finishing his breakfast as Tim came into the kitchen.

'I woke up and I couldn't get back asleep.'

'Are you all right?'

'Yes, I'm fine thanks. Where's Ma?'

'Gone round to Garvey's to buy bread. But there's enough there for your toast. Want some porridge before I go?'

'Yes, please,' said Tim. He smiled reassuringly and sat at the table, but in truth everything wasn't all right and, lying in bed, Tim's thoughts had gone round in circles.

He felt challenged by the idea of trying to catch Wilson red-handedly as he passed over the painting. The anonymous letter had been posted yesterday, and with Dublin's efficient postal service the letter should have reached Superintendent Leech yesterday afternoon. But would he treat it seriously? Or would he dismiss it out of hand, and regard as preposterous the notion of a director of the National Gallery being a thief?

'There you are,' said Da, spooning out the porridge, 'As they used to say when I was a lad – that will put the red neck on you!'

'Grand,' said Tim. He felt a warmth towards his father, knowing that he was trying to cheer him up, despite being under pressure himself from the police and his employers.

'What are you up to this morning, son?' he asked.

'I'm going for a cycle with Deirdre and Joe.'

'Lovely. Where are ye off to?'

'We thought we'd cycle out past Dollymount. Maybe go all the way along the coast and make a day of it.'

Tim felt bad about misleading Da when their destination was Howth, but at least it wasn't a lie to say they would cycle along the coast. The cycle was also as a result of having spent most of his pocket money already on tram fares when following Wilson. Joe had offered to pay for Tim and Deirdre today, but Tim didn't want to take advantage of his friend's generosity. And so he had argued that they should cycle, and that it would give them more freedom of movement when they got to Howth and wanted to observe both the trawler and Furlong's cottage.

'Well, I best be off to the station,' said Da, picking up his lunchbox. 'Enjoy your cycle.'

'Thanks, Da,' answered Tim, waving as his father went out the door. Then he absent-mindedly returned to eating his porridge, as he thought hard about what lay ahead.

* * *

'The high, the low, the sailor's on the sea,

My old man is after me,

Are you going to the fair,

I went, yes, I went, there was no fair there!'

Standing on the street, Deirdre chanted the skipping rhyme as she and Maura Breslin twirled the rope, while Maura's sister Beth lightly skipped to the rhythm. Deirdre was killing time until the agreed early morning rendezvous with Joe. She was nervous yet excited about their mission to Howth today, and she swung the rope and sang the chant mechanically, her mind elsewhere.

The three friends had decided to keep a watch on Furlong's cottage and the trawler, and if they found that the engine was fixed today, then tomorrow's transfer of the stolen painting would surely be on. Deirdre had prayed that the police would act on the anonymous letter they had sent to Superintendent Leech. If not, though, it would be up to them to act, and she was determined to prove that Wilson was the thief, no matter what it took.

'Hello, girls,' said Sadie Nolan now as she approached.

Beth and Maura stopped skipping and greeted her. Deirdre said hello too, even though she wasn't in the mood for Sadie. Since the night of the concert Sadie had changed her attitude a little. Beth and Maura had always been friendly, especially when Sadie wasn't around, and the sisters had praised Deirdre for her performance at the residents' concert. Sadie hadn't congratulated her on her performance, but Deirdre reckoned that she was smart enough not to go openly against the warm response that the neighbours had shown in support of Da.

'So, any news, Deirdre?' Sadie said now, as though concerned.

'About what?'

'The robbery. Have the police been able to clear your father?'

Sadie had said it as though she were sympathetic, but Deirdre felt it was actually a subtle way of getting at her.

'They haven't got the real culprit yet,' she replied.

'That's a shame,' said Sadie, straight-faced. 'Because until they do…well, it's awful, isn't it?'

Deirdre forced herself to keep her temper in check. 'My da will be cleared when they find the real thief,' she said. 'And seeing as you're so interested, Sadie,' she added, unable to keep the sarcasm from her voice, 'you'll be the first person I'll tell. See you, girls,' she said to Beth and Maura, then she nodded to Sadie, turned on her heel and walked away.

* * *

Joe watched as his father buttoned his starched wing-collar and knotted his tie in preparation for going to work. Although it was just after breakfast time, already the June morning was warm, and Joe felt sorry for Dad having to wear such restrictive clothes in the summer. He said nothing, however, knowing that his father was a stickler for what he regarded as the correct attire for his role as a senior clerk. That sort of formality, though, was one of the reasons Joe never wanted to work in somewhere like the Midland Great Western Railway Head Office.

'What are your plans for today, Joseph?' Dad asked now,

making minute adjustments to his tie as he watched himself in the kitchen mirror.

Joe looked up from the breakfast table. 'Going for a bit of a cycle.'

'Where to?'

'Eh…I thought it might be nice to go as far as Howth, seeing as it's so nice.'

'That's quite a long cycle.'

'Sure, I have all day.'

'You haven't forgotten cricket practice this evening?'

Joe hesitated.

'You *had* forgotten, hadn't you?'

'Sorry, Dad, it…it just slipped my mind,' he answered, knowing that he couldn't explain how the task of finding the stolen painting had dominated his thoughts.

'You've a chance to make the first team in the under-fourteen's, Joseph. Don't fritter that away through forgetfulness and lack of commitment.'

'I won't.'

'Who are you going on this cycle with?'

Joe knew that his father wouldn't like the answer, but he didn't want to lie. 'I'm…I'm going with Tim and Deirdre'

'I see.'

Dad had seen the outpouring of support for Mr Kavanagh on the night of the concert, and had applauded himself. But afterwards he had pointed out to Joe that the views of the neighbours would count for nothing with the police, and for very little with the management of the railway, who were deeply upset by the bad publicity the company was getting. Joe knew that his father would prefer if he distanced himself from the Kavanaghs, but in fairness Dad hadn't gone back on his reluctant agreement that he could stay friends with Tim and Deirdre.

'Well, be careful,' he said now.

'I will,' answered Joe, hoping his sense of guilt at lying didn't show. Because if they were to clear Mr Kavanagh's name and expose the real criminals he *couldn't* be too careful, and risks would have to be taken.

'And make sure that you're back in good time for your cricket, all right?'

'OK, Dad,' answered Joe. 'See you this evening.' He waited until his father went out the door, then he turned away, uncomfortable about lying, yet eager suddenly to go into action.

CHAPTER TWELVE

Deirdre felt her pulses starting to race. She had turned left at Howth train station and was cycling towards the pier, closely followed by Tim and Joe. Their trip along the sunlit shoreline of Dublin Bay had been enjoyable, but now Deirdre was oblivious to the picturesque charms of the fishing harbour as she strained her eyes against the sun, seeking out Con Furlong's trawler, the *Bailey Maid*.

Joe had overheard the trawlerman telling Mr Wilson that he would take the vessel for a trial run today, to make sure the engine was properly repaired, and Deirdre wasn't sure whether or not she wanted to see the trawler moored to the quayside. If the boat was gone it meant that the repairs had taken place, and the plan to move the stolen painting would go ahead – with the danger that it might succeed. On the other hand, if the *Bailey Maid* wasn't fixed it just postponed things, and part of Deirdre wanted matters to come to a head.

They cycled along the pier, the scent of fish hanging in the air. It was less busy today than it had been on Saturday, but there were still plenty of people about. Deirdre made sure to keep her demeanour casual, as though she was just out with her friends on a summer cycle.

'There it is!' said Joe, who had the keenest eyesight, 'it's moored at the end.'

'OK, you know what we agreed,' said Deirdre, coming to a halt.

The two boys dismounted and sat on the harbour wall with the air of cyclists who had reached their destination. As Joe had been seen at the cottage by Furlong, Deirdre had suggested that she should be the one to pass close by the trawler, while Tim waited with Joe.

She cycled on, slowing down, but making sure not to stare too obviously as she drew level with the *Bailey Maid*. There seemed to be no activity on board, and Deirdre got a sudden urge to park her bike and check out the trawler. This wasn't part of the plan, but the nearness of the vessel and the absence of any crew made it tempting. She hesitated, quickly weighing things up. If anyone noticed her boarding and challenged her, what would she say? And even if nobody took notice what was to be gained? Wilson wouldn't have transferred the painting yet, and she wasn't interested in any other contraband that Furlong might be smuggling on the trawler.

Deirdre made her decision and cycled on, annoyed at herself for almost giving way to her impulsiveness. Her attention was caught then by a beggar who was sitting against the harbour wall, dressed in a ragged coat despite the summer weather. He had a couple of coins in a battered bowl at his feet and when his eyes met Deirdre's she forgot her own situation and felt a stab of pity. Although she had spent most of her weekly pocket money she reached into her pocket, took out a halfpenny, and dropped it into the bowl.

'God bless you, Miss,' the man said in a hoarse voice.

'You're welcome,' answered Deirdre, then she cycled on to the end of the pier, dismounted, and looked out to sea. She wanted to give the impression of a cyclist relaxing at the end of a spin, but she couldn't shake off the image of the unfortunate beggar. Why was the world run so unfairly that some people had to beg to get by? She knew that she couldn't change things like that, but it still bothered her. Well, at least she could try to tackle the unfairness visited upon her father, she decided.

She hitched up her skirt and mounted the bicycle again. Although she had dressed in a light summer skirt it wasn't as comfortable for cycling as the boys' outfits, but she started back along the pier, determined to stay in Howth all day if need be. She nodded to the beggar as she went past, then she felt her mouth suddenly going dry. A man was coming up on deck on the *Bailey Maid*. In spite of her casual demeanour when she had first passed the vessel, this time she couldn't do the same, and she took a good look at the man.

He was tall, and heavy, and tough-looking, with a small scar on his cheek, and she reckoned that this must be Con Furlong, the man that Joe had encountered at the cottage. The fisherman looked up and caught Deirdre's eye. He had cold, hard eyes, and Deirdre felt a tightening in her stomach. She knew that he could have no idea who she was, and yet she felt deeply uncomfortable.

Then she had passed by, her heart pounding in her chest.

She continued along the pier until she reached the boys. Joe had the binoculars out and was moving his head as though scanning the whole harbour. When he spoke quietly, however, Deirdre realised that he had been watching her.

'So, you saw our friend?'

'That was Furlong?'

'No question,' answered Joe.

'He looks scary.'

'Doesn't he?'

'Did he say anything to you?' asked Joe.

'No, but our eyes met for a second – and it didn't feel good.'

'He's gone back below now,' said Joe.

'This is our chance then,' said Tim. 'Joe and I can check out the cottage while Furlong is on the boat.'

'Be careful, Tim,' said Deirdre.

'We will. And if Furlong starts for home, you can cycle ahead and warn us. All right?'

'All right.'

'Hang on, hang on!' said Joe, his binoculars still trained on the *Bailey Maid*. 'Oh my God!'

'What?' said Deirdre.

'It's smoke. Engine smoke from the trawler!'

'OK,' she said, feeling a tingle of excitement. 'We're on then!'

'And I know you hate us saying it, sis, but I have to,' said Tim.

'I'll get there before you,' said Joe, lowering the binoculars with a grin. 'In the words of Sherlock – the game is afoot!'

Despite herself, Deirdre smiled. 'Just this once I'll go along with you. Because, yes, it looks like the game *is* afoot.'

* * *

A wild goat scampered out of the path of the boys as Tim and Joe rounded a bend in the cliff path. 'Let's hide our bikes in the bracken,' said Tim, 'and do the last bit on foot.'

'Good idea,' answered Joe.

The two boys had cycled from the harbour, then dismounted to climb the steep ascent of Thormanby Road, and now they were on the cliff walk about two hundred yards from Furlong's cottage. They came to a halt and got off the bikes, and Tim glanced around to make sure there were no other walkers nearby.

'Quick, before anyone sees where we've hidden them.'

They lay the bikes down in the bracken, near enough to the cliff walk but still invisible in the dense foliage.

'We'll know where they are from that big rock, it's almost opposite,' said Joe.

'Grand,' said Tim.

They stepped back onto the cliff walk and continued on in the direction of the cottage. Tim could feel his nervousness increasing, but he told himself that if Deirdre had been brave enough to risk breaking into Wilson's house then surely it was his turn to do the same at the fisherman's cottage.

He didn't know what he might find. It seemed most unlikely that the gallery director would have changed his mind and brought the stolen painting to Howth ahead of schedule. There could be other evidence of crime, however, at Furlong's house, and the more evidence that they could uncover for the police the better. The two boys came to an entrance gate, passed through, and walked along the path towards the cottage.

'OK, time to split up,' said Tim. 'Same as before. You blow the whistle if you need to warn me.'

'Sure you don't want me to go in with you?'

'No, better you hide and keep watch.'

'All right. Good luck.'

'Thanks, Joe,' Tim took a deep breath, then made straight for the cottage door. Like Deirdre had done on Iona Road he knocked on the door, hoping to get no reply, but ready to ask for directions if someone other than Furlong was in the cottage. He got no answer. Wanting to be certain, he knocked again, then felt his spirits rising on still getting no response. He went around the corner of the house towards the back door that Joe had described. He hesitated a moment, then got his nerve up and tried the handle of the door. To his relief it was unlocked, and he stepped into the house, but left the door ajar in case he needed to exit quickly.

The room he entered was a kitchen, with dirty dishes stacked haphazardly in the sink and an overflowing ashtray on the table. Stacked on the floor was a pile of cardboard boxes. Tim crossed to them and noticed that the top box had been opened. He lifted the flap on the box and saw that it contained bottles of whiskey. Taking all of the boxes into account there was vastly more whiskey here than could be for personal use. *These were smuggled – or stolen – goods.*

Tim wasn't surprised, and he felt vindicated at more evidence of Furlong's criminal activity. He decided to check the bedroom to see what else he might uncover. If he could find anything written down that connected Wilson to Furlong, he would take it, as evidence to show the police. Just as he was about to leave the kitchen, he heard a sound. Tim swallowed hard and stood unmoving, paralysed with fear.

He had recognised the sound at once as a toilet flushing. It had come from a distance, and he realised that with the kitchen door ajar he must have heard the toilet being flushed in the outhouse. *Which meant the cottage wasn't unoccupied, and if he didn't move quickly he would be caught.* His chest was pounding but he tried to think clearly. If he ran out the door he would come face to face with whoever had flushed the toilet. He had to do something else.

Acting on impulse, he moved in the opposite direction. Off the kitchen there was a tiny corridor with a room on each side, and Tim chose a room at random. He realised that he had stepped into a small parlour, and he closed the door and swiftly went behind a battered sofa. He crouched down in hiding and stayed absolutely still as he heard the back door closing. Barely daring to breathe he prayed that the person who had come in wouldn't enter the parlour. Crouched behind the sofa his eyes scanned the room. It was less untidy than the kitchen, and on the wall there was a large picture of a stag being pursued by hounds, and two photographs. One photograph was of a football team, but the other one sent a shiver down Tim's spine. The picture showed two men, identical in appearance except that one had a small scar, and Tim realised that Con Furlong had an identical twin. Which meant that the one Deirdre had seen at the harbour could have been Con, and the one who flushed the toilet could be his twin brother. Or it could be the other way around.

Before Tim could think any further, he heard footsteps crossing the kitchen. *Please God, let him not come in here*, thought Tim. He stayed perfectly still, afraid to move a muscle, then the steps came into the corridor. Tim felt as though his head would explode from the tension. The footsteps stopped, and Tim heard the person opening the door to the room opposite and stepping in. He breathed out as quietly as he could, and tried to decide what his next move should be. Could he run out while the person was in the other room? It was risky, yet it seemed like his best option.

Taking care not to make a sound, he rose from behind the

sofa. He planted his feet carefully in case of creaky floorboards and began to move forward. Suddenly the parlour door burst open and a heavy-set man with a scar on his face reached out and grabbed him. The man pulled him close then spoke with quiet venom.

'Should have closed the door after you, boy,' he said, then without warning he smacked Tim hard in the face.

Tim fell back against the sofa, but the man grasped his shirt front and drew him near again. Tim's head was spinning, and before he could gather himself the man spoke again.

'What the hell are you up to, son?'

'My...my cat came in your window and I–'

Tim's answer was cut short by another stinging blow, then Furlong drew him near till their faces were only inches apart. 'Don't lie to me, boy. Now tell me what you're at, or by God I'll beat the living daylights out of you!'

* * *

Joe hid behind a thick, overgrown bush at the side of Furlong's garden. He had the referee's whistle in his hand, ready to warn Tim if anyone approached along the garden path. Instead, he was startled to hear his friend shouting 'Get your hands off me!' Joe hesitated, taken completely by surprise. He thought that he would be the one warning Tim of danger – whereas Tim was already in trouble.

Joe waited no longer and moved quickly from behind the bush, trying to make a plan even as he ran towards the front of the cottage.

Joe had definitely seen Furlong at the harbour, so it couldn't be the trawlerman that was accosting Tim. Not that it mattered. Somebody had captured his friend, and he had to save him. Tim had entered the cottage from the rear, so Joe reckoned that the back door was unlocked. He ran towards the front door, deciding that a diversion was needed. He picked up a large stone from the dilapidated rockery. He knew that what he was about to do was illegal, but when he heard Tim roaring, 'let me go!' he had to act. Without any further thought he threw the rock at the window of the front room of the cottage.

Even as the glass shattered, Joe was running at speed around the corner. He had no idea what he would find inside the cottage, but he didn't pause on reaching the back door. He turned the handle and pushed open the door. He guessed that the smashed front window would buy them a few seconds while Tim's assailant would be distracted. He had to make that time count, and he grabbed a frying pan as a possible weapon while crossing the kitchen.

He entered a small corridor. In a second he took in the scene. There were two rooms, one on either side, and both had the doors open. A dazed-looking Tim stood in the room on the left, which looked like a parlour. The sight that met Joe's eyes in the other room made his blood run cold. Picking up the rock from the floor was a rough-looking man. Joe was gobsmacked. He had just seen Furlong on the trawler – yet this man was undoubtedly the person who had opened the door to him and quizzed him on the first reconnaissance of the cottage. *How could he be in two places at once?*

'You!' cried the man in angry recognition.

'Run, Tim! Run!' cried Joe, then he flung the frying pan at Furlong.

The fisherman roared in anger and pain as the pan caught the side of his face. He stumbled backwards, and Joe shouted again for Tim to run. This time his dazed friend obeyed, and Joe slammed the other door shut to buy another couple of seconds. He ran behind Tim, who was moving from the corridor into the kitchen. Joe swiftly followed in his wake but before he got to the back door he heard Furlong bursting out of the front room. From the corner of his eye Joe glimpsed him coming in pursuit. For a big man he moved at speed, and Joe felt a pang of terror. Spurred to move even faster, he crossed the kitchen, banging against a chair that he deliberately toppled after him.

He exited the door and began to sprint down the path, hot on the heels of Tim. Furlong, though, wasn't giving up the chase. Joe heard the trawlerman kicking the chair out of his way, followed by the sound of his footsteps as he ran down the path after them.

Tim flung the garden gate open, then burst out onto the cliff path. Joe followed half a step behind, forcing himself not to lose momentum by looking around. But he could hear Furlong's steps, and he was terrified that he would be caught by the obviously infuriated fisherman.

To Joe's dismay there were no strollers on this section of the cliff path. It meant that if Furlong caught them there was no telling what he might do with no witnesses about. Joe sprinted flat out and drew level with Tim.

'The bikes, Joe!' cried his friend.

Joe could see the rock up ahead opposite which the bicycles were hidden in the bracken. He risked a glance behind and saw that they had pulled away a little from Furlong. *Give up, why can't you?!* thought Joe. But the angry fisherman wasn't giving up.

Suddenly the two boys reached the rock. They strode through the bracken and pulled up the bicycles. Joe's chest felt like it would explode, partly from sprinting and partly from fear as he realised that Furlong was still coming. The trawlerman was panting furiously, but he had closed the gap a little in the time it took the boys to haul the bicycles back onto the cliff path.

'Go, Tim, go!' cried Joe as he ran forward with his bike, placed his foot on the pedal, and hoisted himself onto the saddle. He saw that Tim had done the same, then he pedalled hard, gaining speed. Turning a bend in the path he looked back. Furlong was still on the cliff path. But Joe's heart soared when he saw that the man was doubled over, clearly exhausted and gasping for breath.

'He's stopped, Tim, he's stopped!' Joe shouted jubilantly as he slowed his pace. Then he rounded the bend, lost sight of Furlong, and cycled off down the path.

* * *

The sound of birdsong filled the air, and the sweet scent of gorse was carried on the warm summer breeze. The June sun beat down from a clear blue sky as Tim sat in the shade of an oak tree, in a meadow just off the coast road. He turned to Deirdre and Joe as they settled themselves on the grass. 'OK, let's catch our breath and work out our next move,' he said.

After escaping from the cottage, the two boys had cycled at speed down the steep hill into Howth and picked up Deirdre at the harbour. They had quickly explained what had happened, then cycled towards Sutton Cross, eager to get off the peninsula of Howth and to put some distance between themselves and the Furlong brothers. Having travelled for several miles, they decided it was safe to stop, and had wheeled their bikes through a gap in the hedge that surrounded the meadow.

'Furlong having a twin!' said Deirdre now. 'How did we never think of that, with *us* being twins?'

Tim looked at her impatiently 'Why would we? Just because we're twins, doesn't mean that every time we meet someone, we think they might be a twin too.'

'I was just saying. You don't have to bite my head off!'

'Come on,' said Joe, 'let's not argue. We've had a scare, but we need to calm down and figure out where this leaves us.'

'Yeah...you're right. Sorry, sis.'

'It's OK,' said Deirdre. 'But now that Furlong knows what you two look like, it complicates things.'

'Maybe,' conceded Joe. 'But still, he's no reason to link two twelve-year-old boys to the stolen painting. With a bit of luck, he'll just think Tim was a sneak-thief looking for something to steal.'

'You were dead brave the way you saved me, Joe,' said Tim. 'But that man is dangerous. Are you sure you want to stay involved in this?'

Joe looked his friend in the eye. 'I'm going to pretend I never heard that. We're all in this together, and that's an end to it. All right?'

Tim nodded. 'All right. Thanks, Joe.'

'I was just thinking,' said Deirdre. 'Could we...could we maybe go to the police now? If the cottage is full of cases of whiskey, it'll be obvious that Furlong's a smuggler. Maybe the police would take us more seriously if we tell them Mr Wilson is dealing with a criminal.'

Joe looked unconvinced. 'Even if we went straight to the police, he could have the whiskey moved before they mounted a raid. *If* they mounted a raid. And we still don't have any real evidence to prove that Wilson has the stolen painting.'

'So what do we do?' asked Deirdre.

'Try to catch Wilson red-handed with the painting tomorrow,' answered Tim. 'It'll be harder, now that they know what we look like, and with two Furlongs to deal with, instead of one.'

'So we change our plans to allow for that,' said Joe.

Deirdre nodded. 'Then let's do that.'

'All right,' said Tim. 'Let's work out a new plan.'

CHAPTER THIRTEEN

'Now, second helpings, anyone?' asked Ma cheerily as she approached the dinner table carrying the casserole dish.

'I'll have a small bit more, please,' said Da.

Deirdre watched as her mother ladled out the chicken casserole, then she turned to the twins.

'Tim?'

'No thanks, Ma.'

'Deirdre?'

'No thanks.'

'Sure?'

'Yes.'

Deirdre had said it more sharply than she intended. She had cycled back from Howth with the two boys, and she still felt slightly shaken by the thought of Tim's narrow escape at the cottage. 'I'm fine thanks,' she added, not wanting Ma to know that she was on edge. Deirdre was also becoming frustrated by her mother's relentless cheeriness. She knew that Ma wanted to keep everyone's spirits up while Da was under investigation, but it was starting to irk her. She and Tim weren't babies, and she wished Ma would stop jollying them along.

'I thought all the cycling would have you hungry as a horse,' Ma said.

'Yes, but we had a picnic in Howth,' answered Tim.

'Sure when I was a lad I'd think nothing of having a picnic, and then me dinner,' said Da, 'and then another bit of dinner if it was going! Not that it was often going, sez you.'

Da was speaking in a jovial tone, but Deirdre sensed that this too was a performance.

'With six of us in our family, you thought it was your birthday if you got an extra sausage!' added Ma.

'Oh please!' said Deirdre, unable to stop herself.

'What?'

'Can you just stop pretending, Ma? Can we *all* stop pretending?'

'What are you saying, love?' asked Da.

Deirdre could see that her parents were taken aback, but before she could reply Tim placed a restraining hand on her arm.

'Deirdre,' he said warningly.

'No, Tim, it has to be said. I know it's been awful for you, Da. And Ma, I know you're doing your best, trying to keep things normal. But they're *not* normal. And it's worse having to play along all the time as if they were. Tim and I aren't eejits, we're not babies. You don't have to let on everything is fine.'

'I'm sorry, love,' said Da. 'Ma and I only want what's best for you and Tim. But maybe…maybe you are old enough to know a bit more.'

'Deirdre and I are completely on your side, Da,' said Tim. 'Every step of the way. I think what Deirdre means is that we're all in this together, and it might help to share.'

Deirdre would normally have resented her brother deciding what she meant, but this once she didn't object.

'Fair enough,' said Da. 'What would you like to know?'

'What's happening with the investigation?' asked Deirdre.

'We've all been questioned four times at this stage. Twice by the Midland Great Western Railway, and twice by the police.'

'When you say "we", Da, who are you talking about?' said Tim.

'The driver of the train, me as the guard, the fireman, the two mail clerks, and the station master in Athlone, where we stopped to take on water.'

'So there are six people under suspicion?' said Deirdre,

'Yes, though the mail clerks work for the post office, so the railway company can't put much pressure on them.'

'Are they putting pressure on you, Da?' asked Deirdre. She saw her father look to Ma, who gave a tiny nod of approval.

'Well, seeing as ye want it all out in the open, yes, they have put pressure on me – and the others.'

'What kind of pressure?' queried Tim.

Deirdre saw her father hesitate.

'Tell them, Brendan,' said Ma, 'we've come this far.'

'They've…they've raised the possibility that we could lose our jobs,' said Da quietly.

'And also our house?' said Deirdre.

'Yes, that too,' conceded Da. 'Of course, at this stage it's only a threat. They're trying to frighten whoever *is* the thief.'

'And who do people in the company think that is?'

'I honestly don't know, love. I find it hard to see any of them being guilty. But all I know for certain is that I'm innocent.' Deirdre longed to tell her father about Mr Wilson and Con Furlong, but the three friends had sworn to stick to the original plan of handling things themselves, especially since the police had ignored the anonymous letter.

'So how was it left with the police the last time they questioned you?' asked Tim.

'I was grilled for about an hour by Superintendent Leech. I don't think he believes I did it, but I'd say he wants to keep the pressure on, to see if anyone cracks. So he said I'd be hearing from them again.'

'And what's it like in work?' queried Deirdre.

'The company are doing the same as Superintendent Leech, and putting the people they suspect under pressure to see what happens. But I haven't been suspended, and my workmates are all on my side, so I'm just working away and hoping for the best.'

'And now you know it all,' said Ma. 'All we can do is pray that they catch the real thief.'

Deirdre didn't think that praying was enough, but she said nothing.

'So if there isn't anything else,' said Ma, 'why don't we leave it at that and carry on as best we can?'

'Fine,' said Tim. 'And…thanks for filling us in.'

'Yes, thanks, Ma, thanks, Da', said Deirdre.

Her mother nodded, took up the casserole dish, and made for the scullery.

'Whatever happens we'll get by, don't you worry,' said Da.

'All right, Da,' said Deirdre, then she excused herself and rose from the table. She went out into the scullery and saw that Ma was at the sink. Deirdre couldn't be sure, but she thought she saw a wetness in her mother's eyes.

'Ma?' she said tentatively.

'Yes, love.'

'I'm…I'm sorry for snapping at you.'

Her mother said nothing, but she opened her arms like she used to when Deirdre was younger. Deirdre found herself stepping into her embrace. She felt the warmth of her mother and caught the faint scent of her soap.

'I'm sorry, Ma…I'm really sorry.'

'It's all right, pet. And I'm sorry too. I should have realised that you and Tim have grown up. So not another word about it. Just give me a good long hug.'

Deirdre felt the tears welling in her own eyes and she quickly wiped them away, then wrapped her arms around her mother and held her tightly.

* * *

Joe knelt on the bedroom floor, his head resting on the side of his bed and his hands joined in prayer. Whenever he felt in need he prayed, but not just to God. He had never told anyone, not even Dad, but when he wanted comforting or guidance he sometimes prayed to his dead mother. Nothing was ever going to bring her back, of course, but the idea that she was in Heaven, and still watching out for him, usually made him feel better.

Tonight, though, he was finding it hard to keep his mind on his prayers. It had been such an eventful day that he was still trying to weigh up everything that had happened. He knew that he had disappointed his father. As agreed, they had gone to cricket practice after he got back from Howth. Joe had been tired from the long cycle, though, and after all the drama at the cottage he had found it impossible to concentrate. Dad hadn't criticised him directly, but Joe had picked up on his father's subdued mood on the walk home after cricket practice.

Joe felt bad about disappointing him, yet a part of him felt slightly rebellious. Cricket was *Dad's* favourite sport, not his. It was obviously his father's dream for him to become an accomplished player, but Joe felt he was entitled to prefer soccer and Gaelic football. He enjoyed playing cricket too, but it wasn't his passion, and he wished that Dad could understand that.

Still, there were bigger things to worry about. Even now, hours after the event, he still found the encounter with Con Furlong frightening. He was proud of his role in rescuing Tim. But the thought of what could have happened had he been caught by the thuggish-looking fisherman was terrifying. He could still recall the sound of the man's footsteps in hot pursuit, and he hoped it wouldn't haunt his dreams. It was bad enough having the recurring nightmare about the runaway horse – he didn't need another disturbing image.

At the same time he couldn't deny that he was also excited by how the stolen painting saga was unfolding. He had gone from reading about Sherlock Holmes to being at the centre of a real-life adventure himself. Because of the consequences for Mr Kavanagh, it was no longer a game, and there was no denying that it had become dangerous, yet alongside all of that – perhaps because of it – it was also thrilling.

Joe knew that tomorrow would test his courage, and they would need luck and good timing if their mission was to succeed. Well, there was nothing he could do about that tonight, he decided, and he tried to put it all from his mind. He joined his hands tighter together, conjured up the image of his mother's loving face, and prayed to her for guidance and support.

* * *

Tim tossed and turned, but sleep wouldn't come. Despite being tired after the cycle to Howth and back, his mind was racing. He was relieved that Ma and Da had finally spoken openly about the pressure caused by the police investigation. He wouldn't have had the nerve to speak out like Deirdre had, but he was glad that she had, and that the air had been cleared. It was disturbing, though, that the railway company was hounding Da, and Tim suspected that it could actually be worse than his father had made out. The Midland Great Western Railway might feel it had to be seen to be taking decisive action. Supposing the company sacked Da, and the other three suspects who worked there?

Where would the family go if his father lost his job and his house? Tim knew that many people in Dublin lived in dilapidated tenements where the conditions were appalling, with as many as sixty or seventy people sharing one outside toilet. He hated the idea of his family losing their cosy home, and he felt angry that it was a possibility, when Da was completely innocent. But no sooner would he banish that thought, than his mind would flit to how he had felt when captured by Furlong at the cottage. His roughing up at the hands of the fisherman hadn't lasted for long, but it had been truly frightening at the time. *And what would have happened if Joe hadn't rescued him?* Tim dreaded to think what Furlong might have done. Or supposing Joe hadn't heard him calling out in distress? Or had heard him, but been too frightened to intervene? He was lucky to have a pal like Joe who was brave enough to mount a rescue, and cool enough to smash a window as a diversion.

Now, though, the trawlerman had seen both their faces clearly, which would make things even more difficult tomorrow. Tim had heard the famous quotation that no plan survives first contact with the enemy. It was true, he thought, and already their plan for tomorrow had needed to be re-worked. Going over it again now, Tim found his head buzzing and in frustration he suddenly pulled back the covers and got out of bed.

There was no chance of sleep in this state of mind, and he crossed to the window and quietly pulled the curtain aside so that he could see out. Despite the late hour there was still a glow of light in the blue of the western sky. The window was ajar, and Tim stood still in the darkness of his bedroom, taking deep breaths of the cool night air to steady his nerves.

After a few moments of deep breathing, he sensed that his pulse was slowing, and he felt more in control. When his older sister Anne had left home to work in Cork a few years previously, Tim and Deirdre had each got their own bedroom. Right now, though, with no-one to talk to, he wished that he and Deirdre were back in their old room. *But looking to the past wasn't going to help.* He had to live in the present, prepare as best he could for the future, and hope for the best. Breathing deeply again, he stood unmoving at the window, gazed at the night sky, and wished that morning would come.

PART THREE

SHOWDOWN

CHAPTER FOURTEEN

Deirdre woke with a start. She didn't know what time it was, but her body clock and the sunlight coming around the edge of the curtain told her that she had slept for some time. She had been woken around five a.m. by loud birdsong, but had fallen back asleep, and now she turned in the bed and looked anxiously at the face of her alarm clock. It was ten minutes to seven, and the alarm was about to go in five more minutes.

Deirdre had insisted that Mam have a lie-on today, and that she would prepare Da's breakfast before he went to work. She partly wanted to make up to her mother for snapping at her the previous night, but she also wanted to have a good reason for rising early.

It had been agreed with the boys that she should be the one to watch the cottage in Howth this morning, now that Furlong knew what Tim and Joe looked like. But would Mr Wilson deliver the painting to the cottage, or directly to the trawler at the quayside? There was no means of knowing, and the three friends had decided that both locations needed to be watched.

Deirdre's instinct told her that Wilson would keep gentleman's hours and wouldn't be one for rising early. She couldn't count on that, however, and she wanted to take an early train to Howth. And the sooner she got her father's breakfast organised the sooner she could be on her way. She turned off the alarm on the clock and swung her feet out of bed. Last night she had laid out a fresh white blouse and a summer skirt, and her underwear, stockings, and shoes were neatly arrayed beside them. Reaching for the clothes, she quickly began to dress.

* * *

'I've a surprise for you, Joseph,' said Dad.

Joe paused, a spoonful of creamy porridge halfway to his mouth. It wasn't like his father to go in for surprises, and certainly not over the breakfast table.

'Yes?' said Joe.

'I'm taking a day off.'

'When?'

'Today.'

Joe felt a burst of panic but tried not to show it. *Why did Dad have to pick the day the painting was being moved?* Joe and Tim had planned to track Mr Wilson from Iona Road to Howth and – if the opportunity arose – to snatch the painting from him. And now this had been sprung on him.

'I thought we might go up to the park and do some work on your bowling,' said Dad. 'Maybe a bit of batting too. I know you can play better than you did last night. And after cricket, I thought for a treat we could have a few buns in the Tea Rooms.'

Joe lowered his spoon. 'I eh…I'd love to do that another time,

Dad,' he said, 'but I've already arranged to go to the coast with Tim this morning.' He saw the disappointment in his father's expression, and he felt guilty. But Mr Kavanagh could lose his job, his home, and even his freedom if he went to jail, and that was worse that hurting his father's feelings. 'Sorry, Dad,' he said. 'Can we do it another day?'

'No, Joseph, we can't. I've already taken today off. Do whatever you planed with Tim tomorrow, or on Friday.'

Unable to tell the truth, Joe struggled to come up with a response. 'It's…it's just…'

'Just what?'

'Well…Tim thinks we're meeting this morning.'

'I doubt he keeps a strict social diary, Joseph. Explain I've taken a day's holiday, and you'll see him tomorrow instead.'

Joe's mind was racing, but he didn't know what to say, and before he could mount an argument his father spoke again.

'Now finish up your breakfast, then get your cricket gear organised. All right?'

'Yes, Dad,' he answered, trying not to let his turmoil show. 'All right.'

* * *

'Deirdre, run around to Garvey's, will you, love, and get me a couple of boxes of matches.'

Tim saw the look of concern on his sister's face at their father's sudden request. They had all finished breakfast while Ma had her lie-on, but Tim knew that Deirdre was anxious to get away. As well as the train journey, she also had to travel on the Hill of Howth tram and on foot to reach Furlong's cottage. It had been agreed that she should set off first, and Tim decided now that he had to intervene.

'I'll do it, Da,' he said. 'Deirdre made the breakfast, and I know she's planning now to meet up with the girls.' He made his voice sound casual, not wanting his father to suspect his real motive. Da looked at him. It was unusual for Tim to offer to do a chore for his sister, but then his father shrugged.

'Fair enough.'

'Thanks, Tim,' said his twin, then she moved swiftly to pick up the packed lunch she had made for herself.

'See you later, Da,' she said.

'Bye, love.'

Deirdre gave Tim a surreptitious thumbs up, and he replied with an encouraging nod as she left.

'Now, son,' said Da, reaching into the trouser pocket of his railway uniform and taking out a shilling coin. 'Two boxes of matches. And while you're at it, get yourself a penny's worth of sweets.'

Tim felt a rush of affection for his father, but he wasn't sure how to respond. Normally he would be delighted to get a treat, but with things so uncertain about Da's future he didn't want to be the cause of the family wasting any money. Then again, if he declined the offer he would have to explain why, and that might seem like he wasn't confident that Da's good name would be cleared. And maybe Da needed to feel that he could still spend his hard-earned wages as he saw fit.

Making up his mind, he smiled and reached out for the coin. 'Thanks, Da,' he said. 'Thanks a lot.'

* * *

Deirdre made her way briskly up Monck Place. She was heading for the train station in Drumcondra, and she wanted to get the earliest possible train. Crossing the cobbled roadway, her nose wrinkled from the smell of fresh dung, deposited by one of the many horse-drawn delivery carts that plied their trade around Phibsboro.

She strode ahead, then saw another girl coming along the footpath in her direction. *Sadie Nolan.* Today of all days Deirdre wasn't in the mood for any of Sadie's nonsense. She was surprised to see the other girl out so early, then became even more surprised when Sadie drew nearer, and Deirdre saw her face. Clearly she had been crying, and instinctively Deirdre stopped.

'Deirdre,' said Sadie in a low-key greeting.

'Sadie. Are you all right?'

'Not…not really.'

'What's happened?'

'My…my father…'

'What about him?'

'He's been taken to hospital.'

'What happened him?'

'He got…he got pains in his chest. They said it could be angina – whatever that is. And they took him away in an ambulance.'

'Oh, Sadie, I'm sorry,' said Deirdre.

'I've just come from the church. I've been praying really hard that he'll be all right.'

'I'd say he will be.' Despite how irritating Sadie could be, Deirdre felt sympathetic. 'They'll look after him in hospital, it's the best place for him to be.'

'I suppose.'

'And I'll…I'll say a prayer for him too.'

'Thanks.'

Deirdre wanted to get to the station, but she felt that in the circumstance she couldn't rush off.

'And Deirdre?' said Sadie hesitantly.

'Yes?'

'I'm…I'm sorry. Now that I know what it's like to worry about your father, I should…I should have been nicer to you. Sorry.'

'It's…it's OK. I just hope your da gets better quickly.'

'Thanks. I'll see you.'

'See you.'

Deirdre was relieved that Sadie was the one to end the conversation, and she waited a second or two for decency's sake, then moved off swiftly. She turned right onto Phibsboro Road and made for the busy intersection known as Doyle's Corner. It could be disconcerting when somebody acted out of character, and she was taken aback by Sadie's apology. But genuine as her sympathy was for Sadie's father, she had to have a clear head for what lay ahead today, and she tried to dismiss Mr Nolan from her thoughts.

She crossed over Blaquiere Bridge that spanned the branch line linking the Royal Canal with Broadstone station, then hurried down the North Circular Road, passing the forbidding fortress that was Mountjoy Jail. This was where her father could end up if the false accusation against him was taken to court, and the thought spurred her to carry out her task today.

She reached the busy junction with Dorset Street, noisy even at this early hour with clanking trams, and she turned left, crossed Binns Bridge and made for Drumcondra station. She heard a whistle blast, and saw a plume of steam as a slowing train approached the station. Picking up her pace even more, she ran up the steps of the station, eager to catch the train and finish their mission.

* * *

Joe dreaded having to tell Tim that he wouldn't be with him in Howth this morning. It felt like such a betrayal, despite the fact that he had no choice in the matter. Even as he was organising his cricket gear in the kitchen he racked his brains to come up with a reason to get out of spending the morning with Dad. But try as he might, he couldn't think up anything.

His thoughts were interrupted by a knock on the front door. He hoped it wasn't Tim. At the very least he needed to go to his friend and explain the situation. But Dad had told him to prepare his cricket gear, and he couldn't leave until that was done.

Joe hurried out to the hall, but found that his father had got there before him and was opening the hall door. To Joe's dismay Tim was on the doorstep, and Joe felt awful when he saw his friend's smiling face.

'Good morning, Mr Martin, Joe,' said Tim,

'Good morning,' answered Dad.

'Tim,' said Joe.

'Good timing,' continued Dad, 'we needed a word.'

'Yes?'

'Joseph told me about your plan for today. I'm afraid that can't happen.'

Joe could see that his friend was shocked but trying hard to conceal it.

'Our plan?' said Tim, addressing Dad, but glancing questioningly at Joe.

Joe wanted to tell his friend that he hadn't revealed anything about their secret plan, but before he could speak, Dad carried on.

'Joseph told me what you had in mind. And I understand that you'll be disappointed that I'm intervening.'

Joe could see the beginning of panic on Tim's face, and he knew he had to act before Tim said the wrong thing.

'We can't go on our picnic to the coast, Tim,' he interjected. 'Dad's taken a day off and we're going to the cricket grounds.'

'Oh…right…'

Dad looked slightly taken aback at being cut across, but Joe couldn't worry about that. Instead he imagined his friend's mixed emotions – relief at their secret being safe, but disappointment that Joe would now miss the climax of their mission.

'I took a day's holiday as a surprise for Joseph,' continued Dad. 'Your picnic can wait a day or two I'm sure.'

'Yes, I…yes…it can.'

'Good man,' said Dad. 'I knew you'd understand.'

'We'll…we'll get together as soon as I can,' said Joe, looking Tim directly in the eye and putting an emphasis on the phrase *as soon as I can*. Joe reckoned that he might still be able to get to Howth by early afternoon, and he hoped that his friend would get the coded reference.

'Fine,' said Tim. 'Enjoy your cricket, and…and I'll see you then.'

'Right. See you.'

Dad watched as Tim departed, then closed the hall door. Joe stood in the hallway, unsure of whether or not his friend had understood what he was suggesting.

'All right, Joseph,' said Dad, 'no dilly-dallying. Let's get playing cricket.'

'OK,' said Joe, trying to sound enthusiastic, 'I'll get my gear.'

* * *

Tim stopped as soon as he turned the corner of Great Western Square. He slipped off his rucksack and tried to gather his thoughts. He had been completely unprepared for Mr Martin's sudden cricket project, and he hoped that he hadn't aroused suspicion by looking too taken aback. Falling back on his acting skills, he had done his best to give the impression that his and Joe's plans for today were casual, and Joe's father had seemed to accept that. But he couldn't be sure that he had convinced Mr Martin, and all he could do was trust that Joe managed to keep their real plans for today from his father.

More worrying was the idea of having to carry out their plan without Joe's help. His friend had given a clear hint that he might be able to get to Howth later, but there was every chance that Mr Wilson would want to get the handover to Con Furlong done as soon as possible – which meant that this morning was likely to be the key moment.

Could he do it all himself, if Deirdre was at the cottage, and Wilson showed up at the harbour? *He had to; quitting was out of the question.* But it would be much more difficult. He and Joe had counted on one of them causing a diversion while the other went into action. That wouldn't be possible now. But maybe he could still cause a diversion, and then make his move. He didn't know if he was fooling himself, or if it might actually be practical. Well, there was only one way to find out. He hoisted his rucksack onto his back, turned away from Great Western Square, and set off on his way.

* * *

With a hiss of steam and the screeching of brakes Deirdre's train pulled into Howth station. She had changed platforms at Amiens Street, but neither there nor at Drumcondra had she seen any sign of Mr Wilson. The rail journey, with its occasional views of the sea on a bright summer morning, should have been a pleasure. Deirdre, though, was too tense to savour her surroundings and she stepped from the train with her mind focused on the task ahead.

She glanced at the station clock and calculated that there was a good chance that she was ahead of Mr Wilson. But was he going to the cottage, or directly to the trawler? It was impossible to tell. And which did she want it to be? Part of her would be relieved if the showdown was at the harbour, and the boys dealt with it. But another part of her was angry at how her father had been treated. And Charles Wilson was the person who had caused the trouble by stealing the painting and allowing suspicion to fall on innocent men. Tackling him herself would be deeply satisfying.

It was frightening too, of course, especially if Furlong or his twin brother was at the cottage. And supposing he was sitting outside, taking the summer sun and watching the cliff path? Then she could end up with two adversaries instead of one. *Unless she could intercept Wilson on the path before he got near the cottage.*

Deirdre stepped out of the station and crossed to the stop for the Hill of Howth tram. Her mind was racing, but she tried to marshal her thoughts. She would judge the situation when she got nearer to the cottage and do whatever needed doing. She had deliberately dressed in flat shoes and her lightest skirt and blouse, to allow her to move at speed. She knew what her enemies looked like, but they didn't know her. And she had huge motivation to clear her father's name. All of that ought to be enough to get her through. *It had to be,* she told herself.

Taking a coin from her pocket, she bought a ticket from the conductor of the tram. She mounted the stairs, took an outside seat, and waited impatiently for the vehicle to start its journey up the hill.

* * *

Joe couldn't shake off a double dose of guilt. He was strolling towards the cricket club in the sunny Phoenix Park with Dad, and to a casual observer they must have looked like a father and son off to enjoy a day's sport. But Joe felt really bad at abandoning Tim for the showdown in Howth. He felt bad for Dad too, who thought he was providing a treat by taking a day's leave. It was a nice gesture, and Joe had tried to work up some enthusiasm, but it was a struggle to put Tim's situation from his mind.

Several members exchanged greetings with them as they arrived at Phoenix Cricket Club, then Joe and his father entered the clubhouse. It was the oldest cricket club in the country, and one of its previous members had been the famous politician Charles Stewart Parnell, who had tried so hard to bring about Home Rule for Ireland. Joe, however, was much less interested in the past than he was in the future, and all he could think about was what would happen with his friends later this morning.

Was there any chance that Mr Wilson might leave the transfer of the stolen painting until later in the day – by which time Joe might be able to get to Howth? Even as he posed the question, Joe thought he knew the answer. If it were him, he would be eager to get rid of the stolen item as soon as possible. Which meant that even if he got to Howth in the early afternoon, the chances were that it would be too late.

'All right, Joseph,' said Dad. 'Let's get changed, then we'll get working on your bowling.

Joe forced himself to smile. 'OK, Dad. Sounds good…'

* * *

Deirdre looked ahead impatiently as the tram trundled up the incline of Howth Head. She had no interest today in watching out for wild goats or gazing at the distant outline of the Mountains of Mourne. Now that the day of reckoning was here, she wanted things to come to a head, one way or another. The plan was to seize the painting, either at the harbour or up at the cottage, and immediately bring it to the police station in Howth. It had been decided that Joe alone should hand it over to the police. He was an independent witness who wasn't related to any of the suspected railway staff who were present on the night of the theft, and he could give sworn testimony that Wilson and the Furlongs had been partners in crime.

She still felt daunted, though, by what she would need to do if Wilson came to the cottage rather than the harbour. To bolster her courage she had listed in her head the advantages she had, and she recalled them now to try to stiffen her resolve. *She would have the element of surprise. She was a twelve-year-old girl, and when they saw her, they would almost certainly under-estimate her. She was capable of being daring and cool under pressure, as she had proven during her burglary of Wilson's house.*

But as the tram began to slow down on approaching the

summit, Deirdre felt uncertain. This would be different to break-ing into an empty house. This was pitting herself against a grown man – maybe two grown men – and what if they were just too much for her? *No!* she thought, she couldn't afford to entertain doubts or she would paralyse herself. She loved Da dearly and she would do anything – *anything* – to prove his innocence. As the tram clanked to a halt she rose determinedly from her seat and started down the stairs.

* * *

Tim stood on the platform of Drumcondra station scanning the faces of his fellow passengers as they awaited the train. It was possible that Mr Wilson might show up at this, his local station. And if he was carrying a package that looked like the rolled-up painting, Tim could strike here and now. But even as he observed each new arrival on the platform Tim sensed that that was too much to hope for.

He had considered waiting outside Wilson's home and trail-ing him from there. But he had dismissed the idea, feeling that he would have looked too obvious while standing alone on Iona Road. Tim feared too that Wilson might not walk to Drumcon-dra station, but might take a cab from his house to Amiens Street to get a direct connection to Howth. In which case he would have lost his man and might not have caught up with him before he got to his rendezvous with Con Furlong.

By taking an early train Tim reckoned that he should get to the harbour before Wilson. He had gone over and over in his head how he might adapt the original plan that he had worked out with Joe. A lot would depend on how events unfolded at the trawler. He glanced down at his rucksack, that he had slipped off his back. There was the faintest smell of paraffin from the sealed bottle that he had placed at the top of the rucksack, as far away as possible from his packed lunch. But would he really have the nerve to use it the way he and Joe had planned?

Maybe he wouldn't need to if he was lucky. Then again, they had already used up quite a bit of their luck, what with Deirdre evading the housekeeper during the break-in, Joe talking his way out of trouble on first encountering Furlong, and Tim himself being rescued and escaping on his bicycle. Maybe at this stage they were pushing their luck. But there was no turning back now. *He had to see this through – and hope their luck held one more time…*

* * *

Joe tried to stay patient as his father stood in the pavilion chatting to the club president. Dad was always highly respectful of anyone in authority, and when the older man had stopped to talk to Dad about a fund-raising event, Tim knew his father would listen for as long as the president wanted.

Tim was already frustrated at not getting to support Deirdre and Tim, but he knew that Dad would expect him to be polite, and so he tried not to let any impatience show. Now though his heart sank when the president suggested to Dad they look at some figures in a ledger kept in the committee room.

'Why don't you head in and change, Joseph?' said his father. 'I'll join you presently.'

'All right, Dad,' he replied. Joe entered the changing rooms and laid down his cricket gear on one of the wooden benches. He sat and tried to come to terms with the turmoil that still gripped him. For the first time since Tim had called to the house he was alone and didn't have to put on a false face, and it was a relief to be able to acknowledge his feelings, however topsy-turvy they were.

No matter what way he looked at it, though, to be practising his spin bowling or improving his batting seemed really wrong when his friends needed help. How could he ever look Tim in the eye if Mr Kavanagh went to prison? How could he explain to Deirdre that he was working on his cricket, and eating buns in the Tea Rooms, on the day that she and Tim were set to tackle Wilson and Furlong? Yet what choice did he have?

Reluctantly he opened his kit bag and took out his cricket shirt. He rose to get dressed, then stopped. He had never felt so torn in his life, and he stood immobile. After a moment he made up his mind. He couldn't live with himself if he was missing when his friends needed him most. *He had to get to Howth.* Moving quickly, before he lost his nerve, he threw the cricket shirt down. He scribbled a note saying 'Sorry, Dad, I had to go. See you later,' placed the note on top of his kit bag, and made for the changing room door.

He opened the door and carefully peered out. There was no sign of Dad or the club president, and Joe stepped out. He walked briskly from the clubhouse, but not so fast as to draw attention. Reaching the track that led to the main road of the park, he began to run.

He knew that there would be hell to pay for this, but he didn't care. Putting from his mind all thoughts of his father, and the consequences of what he was doing, he picked up his pace, heading for the entrance to the park and the way into town.

* * *

Laughter and lively conversation could be heard from the beer garden of the Summit Inn as Deirdre walked past. A warm wind was blowing, but otherwise it was shaping up to be a glorious summer day, with clear blue skies, and the fine weather had brought people out in numbers. It seemed unfair to Deirdre that others should be so carefree when she was so worried. No sooner had she thought it than she admonished herself. Lots of these people probably had worries of their own. And everyone lived to some extent in their own little bubble of family and friends. The problem, she knew, wasn't other people being carefree. The problem was that Deirdre's bubble was shortly going to collide with that of a group of criminals, and she was frightened.

Well, that was only natural, she thought, as she left the beer garden behind and reached the viewing point at the summit. Despite her nervousness she couldn't help but be taken by the view across Dublin Bay. She saw the picturesque Bailey Lighthouse standing like a sentinel at the entrance of the bay, and rising as a backdrop against the opposite shoreline were the peaks of the Dublin and Wicklow mountains.

She looked at the pointed cone of the Sugarloaf Mountain, and it brought back memories of a day out that the family had spent there last summer during Dad's holidays. They had taken a train to Bray, then a jaunting car to the base of the Sugarloaf, and Tim and Deirdre had raced up the final steep section to the mountain peak. They had all revelled in the panoramic view, had a delicious picnic that Ma had made, and sang songs on the way back to Bray in the jaunting car.

The memory made Deirdre wistful now, and she turned her back on the view and started along the cliff path. She looked across the green of the cliff tops to the sparkling sea, and smelled the sweet scent of gorse, and she told herself that life would be good again, and that this time too would pass. She knew that if you wanted to succeed with most things, you had to believe that you *could* succeed, and so she told herself firmly that today's mission would be accomplished.

Her resolve hardened, she picked up her pace, eager to get near to Furlong's cottage. Then she would find a hiding place, lie in wait for Mr Wilson, and strike when the moment was right.

* * *

Tim clutched his ticket tightly as he stepped away from the ticket office in Amiens Street station. He had spent the last of his pocket money buying a return ticket to Howth, and if he lost or misplaced the ticket he couldn't afford another one.

Stop fretting, he thought, there would be bigger things to worry about when he got to the harbour. Looking at the arrivals and departures board, he saw that his train wasn't due for another fifteen minutes, and so he took a seat in the busy station concourse.

In one way the waiting was agony, while another part of him never wanted the train to arrive. He was scared of what lay ahead, and the thought that if it backfired he could get arrested. He could even end up in a juvenile detention centre. Tim had heard whispered stories of the brutal punishments inflicted on boys who were sent away to reformatories, and he worried about how he would survive in such a place. He wasn't the fearless type, wasn't the kind of daring boy who walked along the top of walls, oblivious to danger. In fact he had recently baulked and walked away when several of the local boys had challenged him to join them in dropping down to the ground from a high wall. So would his nerve fail him today if he needed to do something really brave? He hoped not. But he wasn't sure, and his thoughts went round in circles as he anxiously awaited his train.

* * *

Joe's chest had finally stopped heaving, and he was glad to sit back in his seat as his tram rattled along the quays towards town. He had boarded the tram at its terminus outside the gates of the Phoenix Park after he had run all the way from the cricket grounds. He had arrived at the tram stop gasping for oxygen, and queasy from gulping in air that carried a strong smell from the nearby Guinness Brewery. Now, though, as the vehicle sped towards the city centre, the enormity of what he had done was sinking in. He had never before blatantly disobeyed his father, who would be worried about him. Too late to fret about that now, he thought. If he was to help Tim he needed to forget about Dad for the time being, and focus all his energy on getting back the stolen painting.

He willed the tram to go faster as it travelled down the quays, beside which the River Liffey's waters sparkled in the warm June sunshine. Finally the tram reached the bustling centre of the city, and Joe quickly alighted. He briefly considered making for Tara Street station. Although on the far side of the river, it was actually nearer than Amiens Street. But if Mr Wilson was travelling by train he would go from Drumcondra and change in Amiens Street. Joe was still open to the possibility of intercepting Wilson, and if he was carrying an obvious package that could be snatched, then a showdown in Howth might be avoided. *So Amiens Street it was.*

Joe ran past Liberty Hall, the union headquarters, and around by the back of the imposing Custom House, making for the station. Weaving through the busy horse-drawn traffic on Amiens Street, he was almost hit by a baker's carriage, and the driver shouted and cracked his whip in Joe's direction.

'Sorry!' Joe shouted back without breaking stride. He reached the station and, summoning up his last reserves of energy, ran up the steps and into the building.

He joined the queue at the ticket window. By the time he reached the top of the queue his breathing was returning to normal, and he bought a ticket for Howth, then headed out onto the station concourse.

He scanned his surroundings, hoping he might spot Mr Wilson. But there was no sign of the gallery director. It was what Joe expected, but he still felt a little disappointed. Then he stopped dead. Less than twenty yards away was a sight that gave his heart a lift. Sitting on a bench was Tim, who hadn't seen him yet. Joe crossed over and stood before him. 'Hello. stranger,' he said.

Tim looked up in amazement. 'Joe? You…you got away!'

'Yes.'

'Boy, am I glad to see you! How…how did you change your dad's mind?'

'I was never going to change his mind. So, I ran away.'

'Oh, God, Joe, you didn't?!'

'I couldn't leave you in the lurch. So, here I am.'

Tim seemed lost for words, and Joe could see that he was moved.

Eventually Tim spoke softly. 'You're …you're a brilliant friend, Joe.'

'You're not so bad yourself.'

'But what will happen with your dad?'

'We'll worry about that tonight. Today we've other things to deal with.'

'Yeah…'

'And I think this is our train,' said Joe as a steam-spewing locomotive pulled up to one of the platforms. 'Looks like I just made it in time.'

'I'm really glad you did.'

'I am too,' said Joe. 'We've come this far together – we might as well go the whole way.'

'Will I say it, or will you?' asked Tim,

'I'll say it, Sherlock,' answered Joe with a mile. 'The game is afoot.'

'The game is afoot,' echoed Tim.

CHAPTER FIFTEEN

Deirdre was dazzled by the bright June sunshine, and she raised her hand to shield her eyes. She was looking almost directly into the sun as she watched the bend in the cliff path from her hiding place in the bracken. She had crouched down on her hunkers, her eyes level with the top of the bracken, and time had passed slowly.

Maybe Wilson had gone directly to the *Bailey Maid*, she thought, and all the action would be at the harbour. No sooner had she thought it than she saw another walker coming around the bend. She strained her eyes, moving her hand lower down her forehead, the better to shield herself from the glare. She had already had two false alarms, with walkers that she initially thought might be Wilson, but despite herself, she now felt a tremor of excitement as the latest man drew nearer. He looked to be about the same height and build as the gallery director. He was wearing a straw hat and what looked like well-cut summer clothes, and he carried a cylindrical container at his side. Was this really him, bearing the rolled-up painting?

The man walked at a moderate pace, a little faster than most strollers, and Deirdre felt her heart beginning to race. Drawing closer, he glanced to the right, taking in the sea view. In turning his face, he had been fully visible, and Deirdre felt her pulses racing. *It was Wilson, no question.* And the container must surely hold the stolen painting. Finally, the waiting was over. She took a deep breath and paused a moment. Then she breathed out, and rose from the bracken.

* * *

Tim waited impatiently at the carriage door, then pulled the handle to open it before the train had shuddered to a halt in Howth station. He alighted quickly, with Joe at his heels, and they made for the exit. The smell of engine smoke from the station mixed with the harbour scent of fish and sea air as the two boys reached the corner and looked down the pier. Tim prayed that the *Bailey Maid* would be at its berth, and that the trawler wouldn't have left early for any reason. This time Joe didn't have his father's binoculars, and both boys strained their eyes against the harsh sunlight.

'I see it!' cried Joe.

His friend had always had the better eyesight, and it was only when they had gone a little further that Tim could see the trawler for himself.

'OK,' he said. 'Let's not go too near.'

'We can sit down on the wall, out of the way, and keep a watch,' suggested Joe.

'Fine,' said Tim, joining his friend as he sat on the harbour wall. He was aware that Con Furlong now knew what he and

Joe looked like, and that they would have to be careful. Tim had brought a sun hat and children's sunglasses, that he donned now with the intention of at least partially disguising himself.

'Oh,' said Joe, 'now that we're here…'

'What?

'I feel…I feel pretty nervous. Do you?'

'Dead nervous,' admitted Tim. 'But also…also determined to see it through.'

'Me too.'

'I was thinking about it. I reckon there are three things that can happen.'

'What are they?' asked Joe.

'Well, the best one is that Deirdre gets to Wilson on his way to the cottage. It's the least public place, and if she snatches the painting from him and gets away that would be perfect.'

'What's the second thing?' asked Joe.

'Next best is that we intercept Wilson here, and escape with the painting.'

'And the third thing?'

'Wilson goes to the cottage, but Deirdre doesn't get to him. That would mean Furlong, instead of Wilson, bringing the painting down here. But Furlong knows what we look like. So, it would mean taking it from someone who can recognise us.'

'Right,' said Joe. 'But we still have our diversion plan.'

'We do.'

'That's it then. There's nothing more we can do for now, is there?'

'No,' said Tim. 'We have to just bide our time.'

* * *

Deirdre had carefully timed her move out of the bracken. She didn't want to startle Mr Wilson by stepping suddenly onto the cliff path before him. Instead she moved as though strolling back to the path after taking a diversion. To her relief nobody else had come around the bend after Wilson. As he drew nearer she could see from his face that he looked tense. But he surely wouldn't see the approach of a twelve-year-old girl as a threat. *Would he? Make yourself look harmless*, she thought.

Deirdre forced a smile onto her face as they drew closer, and she nodded in greeting. All the while, though, her focus was actually on the cylindrical container that Wilson carried by his side. He didn't return her nodded greeting, his attention on the trail ahead, then just as they went to pass each other Deirdre made a grab. She could see that she had taken him completely by surprise, and she snatched the container from his hand.

'No!' he shouted, but Deirdre looped her hand through the leather strap of the cylindrical container, grasping it firmly as she turned away. She swung around, intending to run away along the cliff path. To her shock the way was blocked by a tall, heavy man.

In her total focus on Wilson's approach she hadn't looked behind her. Now the man moved at speed, grabbing Deirdre and pulling her closer.

'Little brat!' he said, 'I'll show you!'

'No!' cried Deirdre. She realised that the man was one of the Furlong brothers, then felt a jolt in her arm as he reefed the container from her grip with one hand. She saw him swinging his other hand in a quick arching motion, and she jerked back. But the speed of his attack was too fast for her, and his fist connected with the side of her head. Instantly everything went black, and she fell to the ground.

* * *

'I've just thought of something,' said Joe.

'Yes?'

'We could end up being outnumbered.'

Tim sat up straighter on the sunlit harbour wall and looked at his friend. 'How?'

'If it's just Wilson who shows up here with the painting, then fine, we outnumber him two to one. But if Furlong arrives with him, or comes off the boat and waits for him on the pier, then it's two each.'

'We still wouldn't be outnumbered.'

'We would be if there were three of them.'

'Who'd be the third?'

'Maybe Furlong's twin brother – if he's already on the boat? Or maybe…'

'What?'

'You might think this sounds a bit mad. But I've been looking down the pier with nothing to do except think.'

'And?'

Joe shrugged. 'And I've been thinking about that beggar. He was sitting on the quayside the last day, and he's sitting here again today. Just supposing…supposing he isn't really a beggar? That he's one of Furlong's men? Keeping a watch on everything?'

'Gosh,' said Tim. 'That never even entered my head. But… would they go to all that trouble? Have someone sit there in disguise all day?'

'They might if this deal means a lot to them.'

'But it's not like the painting is stored on the trawler, and he's protecting it.'

'That's true,' conceded Joe. 'Maybe you're right. Maybe I'm letting my imagination run away with me.'

'Either way,' said Tim, 'we know what we need to do. We can't change what they do, so let's just concentrate on our own plan.'

'You're right,' said Joe. 'I just want things to come to a head. Meanwhile, let's go through the plan one more time.'

* * *

Deirdre spluttered as a bucket of cold water was thrown into her face. She came to with a jolt and found that her head was throbbing with a splitting headache. She blinked her eyes rapidly and realised that she was in somebody's house, with the curtains shutting out most of the bright morning light. The room had a stuffy atmosphere and Deirdre instinctively felt the need for fresh air. She tried to rise from the chair on which she found herself. To her horror, she realised that she couldn't move. She felt a stab of panic as she discovered that her arms and feet were tied to the chair.

'Let me go!' she cried, even though she couldn't see anyone in the room.

'Shut up,' answered a deep voice from behind her, 'unless you want me to give you another thump.'

Deirdre felt really frightened, yet part of her was also outraged. 'Go ahead, you big coward! she said. 'No proper man would hit a girl!'

'You want to watch that mouth of yours. Nobody can hear you here, and nobody's coming to find you. So don't force me to put manners on you.'

Deirdre thought it best to say nothing, but her mind was racing as she tried to work out what had happened. She reckoned that her captor must have been waiting in the cottage, but had come out as Wilson had approached. She had been so intent on timing the snatch from the gallery director that she hadn't realised that she had been spotted from behind. So, where was she now? Back in the cottage, presumably. Before she could think any further, the man came around into her line of vision. The trawlerman was big, unshaven, and with cold, piercing eyes. Noting the absence of a scar, Deirdre realised that this must be Con Furlong.

'I don't like nosy brats,' he said, 'so you better tell me, and quickly, what your game is.'

Despite her fear, Deirdre's instincts told her not to show weakness, and that attack might be the best form of defence. 'What's my game?' she said, making her voice sound as strong as possible. 'It's more a case of what's *your* game? And the answer's robbery. Well, the game is up, mister.' Deirdre saw that Furlong looked taken aback, and she decided to press further 'No sign of Mr Wilson anywhere about. Scared off, is he?'

'How the hell are you involved in this?!'

'My father's a train guard, and he's accused of being a criminal. But he's not a criminal – you are. And this time you're not getting away with it.' Deirdre knew that she had to bluff now, and she looked Furlong straight in the eye. 'The police know what's going on.'

There was a short pause.

'The police know, do they?' he answered, with an air of confidence that Deirdre didn't like.

'Yes, they do.'

'Then where are they? Why amn't I under arrest?'

When Deirdre didn't answer immediately, he smirked. 'You never told them, did you? You're just playing at cops and robbers with those other two kids.'

'I don't know any other two kids.'

'Lie away, it makes no difference. None of you went to the police. You know that you've no evidence. That they wouldn't take a kid seriously and you'd be laughed out of it.'

Deirdre thought for moment, then spoke slowly, trying to sound calm despite her fear. 'You're right,' she said. 'I didn't go to the police. I knew that once they saw me it would be like you said. So instead I wrote a letter. A letter telling them all about you, and Mr Wilson, and the *Bailey Maid*.'

There was another pause, then Furlong spoke in a low, angry voice. 'You really shouldn't have done that.'

'But I did. So the game is up. And the smart thing now for you, would be to quit while you still can.'

'I won't be quitting,' he said, 'you can forget that. 'But as for you – you've just made yourself into a problem.'

* * *

Tim kicked his feet restlessly against the harbour wall, then turned to his friend. 'Let's put our minds at rest,' he said.

Joe looked at him questioningly 'How?'

'With the sunglasses and the hat on, I look different to the other day. Why don't I do a quick recce down the pier?'

'What for?'

'I could take a better look at the beggar. Try and figure out if he's genuine. And maybe see if anything is happening at the boat?'

'Supposing Wilson arrives while you're gone?'

'You just fall in behind him, I see you both coming, and we still follow our plan.'

'I don't know, Tim...'

'Doing nothing is killing me. And the beggar thing is playing on my mind.'

'All right,' said Joe reluctantly. 'But be really careful.'

'I will, I promise.'

Tim hoisted himself up off the harbour wall, then started down the pier. He made sure to seem as if he were just sauntering along, even though his pulses were racing. He looked with apparent interest over the edge of the harbour wall at other trawlers that he passed, then drew closer to the *Bailey Maid*. He saw that the beggar was seated with his back against the far wall and that he had a bowl containing coins in front of him. Although the sunglasses shielded his eyes, Tim still tried not to appear to stare at the man as he walked past. Surreptitiously, though, he took in as much about him as possible, from his ragged clothes to his broken boots, to his vacant-looking expression. As he passed the man he heard the throb of a motor and, switching his glance back towards the harbour, Tim realised that it was the *Bailey*

Maid whose engine was running. There was no-one on deck, and the boat was still tied to the capstans on the quayside with thick ropes, but the running engine meant one thing to Tim. The vessel was ready to depart, and once the painting was on board Con Furlong could make a fast getaway. Tim sensed that things were going to come to a head, and with his heart thumping, he hoped once more that his nerve wouldn't fail him.

He walked on a little further so as not to make obvious his interest in the *Bailey Maid*, then he casually turned as though having strolled enough, and started back along the pier.

* * *

Deirdre chafed at the ropes binding her to the chair. No matter what way she tried to move her hands, however, she couldn't do anything to loosen her bonds. Her clothes felt soaking wet from when Furlong had thrown the water into her face, but she tried to put aside her discomfort and focus on what was happening around her. At the edge of her vision she could see her captor pulling up the threadbare and stained carpet that covered the floor. Eventually she could contain her curiosity no longer and she swivelled her head towards him. 'What are you doing?' she asked.

'Goin' to take you on a magic carpet ride.'

'What?'

'This will wrap you up nicely,' he said, rolling out the expanse of carpet on the floor. 'And then I'll take you on little pleasure cruise. And if you give me any trouble – any trouble at all – you'll end up at the bottom of the sea.'

Deirdre sensed that he actually meant it. 'You'd…You'd kill me over a painting?'

'Only if I have to.'

'You'd never get away with it. My brother knows I was watching your cottage.'

'Makes no difference. If you cross me, you'll vanish without a trace. But if all goes well, we'll do our business at sea, and after that you're no threat to me.'

Deirdre badly wanted to believe him, but she wasn't sure she could. 'And you'll just release me?' she said, trying to keep the desperation out of her voice

'I can afford to. You haven't a shred of proof. There's nothing linking the painting to Wilson or me. You're just a hysterical kid with a wild imagination, who needs to frame someone else to clear her father.'

'That's a filthy lie!' snapped Deirdre.

'But you can't prove it. And now, I've heard enough of your guff. Time to shut you up.'

Furlong advanced with a large handkerchief, which he started to wrap around Deirdre's mouth.

'No!' she cried, her voice suddenly muffled as he pulled the handkerchief tight from behind and knotted it. She screamed another muffled 'no', but he ignored her. Instead he untied her from the chair, then forced her to the ground, retying her hands and feet. Even though she knew what was coming she had to fight a wave of claustrophobia when Furlong rolled her up inside the dark, smelly carpet. She felt him tying it at the top and bottom, then she was hoisted up into the air, helpless to resist as he carried her towards the door.

* * *

'You're making too much of this beggar thing,' said Joe, as he and Tim sat together again on the harbour wall.

'You can't know that.'

'Why not?'

'Because you weren't there,' said Tim testily. 'I got within ten feet of him.'

'I saw him the other day.'

'But you weren't examining him then the way I just have.'

'And what, he looks a bit young for a beggar, so you think he's one of Furlong's men?'

'I didn't say he definitely was. But most of the beggars I've seen look old, and this fella looked young. So we need to be on our guard, all right?'

'OK, Tim, OK.'

'Sorry. I'm…I'm just a bit edgy.'

'It's all right,' said Joe, 'we both are. But we're on the same side, so let's not argue.'

'Yeah.'

It was rare for the two friends to disagree, and Joe knew it was the tension of waiting so long, yet having to be on the alert and ready to go into action at short notice. 'Just think, this will all be worth it,' he said, 'if we get the painting back and clear your da's name. Let's concentrate on that.'

'You're right. Though for good measure, I'd love to see Wilson behind bars.'

'He deserves it for what he's put innocent people through.'

'And the trawlermen should be arrested. If it wasn't for what they're…'

'What?' asked Joe when his friend never finished the sentence.

'Don't…Don't turn around and stare,' said Tim who had glanced back towards the entrance to the pier.

Joe felt a surge of excitement. 'Is it Wilson?'

'No. Something we weren't expecting. A horse and cart.'

'Who's in it?'

'Furlong,' Tim answered, a tremor in his voice.

'This is it then,' said Joe. 'This is it!'

* * *

Deirdre was bumped as the cart travelled along the quayside, with the smell of fish alerting her to the fact that they had reached the harbour. Furlong had bundled the carpet that she was wrapped in onto the floor of the cart, and the journey from the cottage to Howth village had been hot, claustrophobic and deeply uncomfortable. Deirdre had tried to loosen the rope binding her wrists without success, although she had gained a little slack in the binding at her ankles. But if she was going to try to kick to draw attention, the place should be at the *Bailey Maid* when – she hoped – Tim and Joe would be present.

When Furlong had questioned her earlier she had been careful to play down the role of the boys, and had striven to give her captor the idea that she was the one trying to prove her father's innocence, and that she was acting alone today. She couldn't deny the boys' role in the incident at the cottage, but she had tried to make out that she had pressurised them into scouting it out on her orders. She had further pushed the notion that she had broken into Wilson's house alone, from which she had made the link to Furlong and the *Bailey Maid*.

She wanted to give Tim and Joe the best possible chance of striking unexpectedly at the quayside, although she wasn't sure how much of her story Furlong had believed. More worryingly, she wasn't sure if Furlong was telling the truth when he said that he would release her after successfully offloading the stolen painting.

Presumably he was transferring it to a bigger vessel at sea, perhaps one travelling to the continent. Or maybe the trawler was to transport it to England. Either way, would he really keep his word and release her? The alternative was too frightening to think about, and she had forced herself not to dwell on it.

Sensing now that they would soon be at the *Bailey Maid,* she tried to ready herself for action. The gag prevented her from screaming, but maybe when she was being unloaded from the cart she could still make some sound and kick as forcefully as her leg bindings allowed. It wasn't a great plan, and she couldn't be sure that it would attract the attention of Tim and Joe. But it was all that she could come up with – and she prayed that it would be enough.

* * *

Tim's mind was racing. Now that the waiting was over things were happening fast. He could see Furlong sitting up on the approaching cart, but there was no sign of Wilson. Had the gallery director delivered the painting to the cottage? And if so, what had Deirdre done? And where was she now?

'Be ready with the paraffin!' said Joe, breaking into his thoughts.

'I will. But keep our backs turned till he's gone past.'

'OK!'

Tim hoped his sister was all right. He told himself that she was probably making her way back down to the harbour on foot, which would explain Furlong arriving before her. Though perhaps Furlong wasn't actually taking the painting on board right now. But Tim's instincts told him that he was, and he opened his rucksack, his hands trembling as he reached for the bottle of paraffin oil.

* * *

Deirdre was jolted as the cart came to a halt. She could feel the perspiration running into her eyes as she lay bound up inside the hot, dark carpet. Her heart was pounding, and her mouth had gone dry, but she knew that she mustn't panic. She had to keep her wits about her if she was to get her timing right and draw attention. Kick and wriggle too soon, and no-one was likely to see her in the cart. Leave it too late, and Furlong would have her on the boat and out of public view. There would be a brief window when he had to lift her from the floor of the cart and carry the rolled-up carpet across the pier, and that was when she had to kick and buck as wildly as she could.

She lay still, conserving her energy. Would Furlong transfer the painting first? If he did, she needed to resist the temptation to make her move too soon. Or maybe his instinct would be to get her out of the way as quickly as possible. Either way she had to be ready, and hope that Tim and Joe weren't fooled by the rolled-up carpet. Before she could fret about it any further, she heard Furlong jumping down onto the quayside. Then she suddenly found herself being lifted into the air as her captor slung the carpet over his shoulder.

* * *

Joe pulled open his box of matches. It had been Tim's idea to create a diversion by starting a fire, and Joe could see that his friend was ready to smash the bottle of paraffin oil on the flagstones of the quayside. Paraffin oil was highly inflammable, but it was also in regular use in home heaters, and there had been no difficulty in getting it at their local hardware store. The boys had quickly followed the cart along the pier to where the *Bailey Maid* was moored, unseen by Furlong who had his back to them. The plan had been to smash the bottle of paraffin and set it ablaze just as Furlong tried to transfer the painting onto the boat. In the confusion Joe hoped to snatch whatever container the painting was in and sprint off down the pier. Although he was a fast runner and confident that he could outpace Furlong, the plan depended upon split second timing, and also on Furlong storing the rolled-up painting in an identifiable container. Joe was fairly confident that they would spot the container, but the timing was likely to be more of a challenge.

Now, though, Joe was stopped in his tracks by what he saw.

Instead of transferring a small container, as the boys had been expecting, Furlong had hoisted a large roll of carpet onto his shoulders. And as the man moved towards the *Bailey Maid* there was movement and a muffled sound from inside the carpet.

'Oh, no!' said Joe, 'There's…there's someone inside it!'

Just then Furlong's twin brother appeared on deck and reached out his hands, ready to receive the carpet. Joe was in shock, but his brain was still working. There was a logical answer to what was going on – and it horrified him. Deirdre had gone missing at Furlong's cottage, and now someone of about her size was being bundled onto Furlong's boat.

'It's Deirdre!' he cried, pointing to the handover of the carpet. 'They've taken Deirdre!'

* * *

Tim was dumbfounded, but he saw the movement in the carpet as Furlong passed it over the rail of the ship to his twin brother. 'No!' he cried. The plan had been to remain unseen until the moment when the painting was produced. But none of that mattered as much as the safety of his sister, and Tim couldn't control his gut reaction. 'No!' he shouted again, then he threw the bottle down onto the quayside, smashing it to pieces. There was a strong smell of paraffin oil, and Joe immediately struck a match and chucked it onto the spreading pool of oil. There was a whoosh of flames, and Tim felt the heat from the burning liquid. From the corner of his eye he saw the beggar rising to his feet, and now the man retreated hurriedly as the flaming paraffin flowed across the quayside.

The carthorse reared up, terrified by the sudden flames, and for Tim time seemed to stand still as he locked eyes with Furlong. Tim saw the recognition in the fisherman's eyes. Then Furlong moved quickly back towards the cart, shouting, 'Cast off, Mick!' over his shoulder. The horse reared up again, whinnying loudly as the spreading flames got nearer to him, and this time the animal almost toppled the cart.

The vehicle landed with a thud, and immediately Furlong reacted. He grabbed a cylindrical container from the floor of the cart and quickly hoisted it free. Everyone else in the vicinity was distracted by the chaos of the raging fire and the panicked horse, but Tim and Joe both sprang forward. Tim made for the rail of the trawler with Deirdre as his priority, while from the corner of his eye he saw Joe grappling with Furlong.

Tim vaulted over the low rail of the boat and landed awkwardly. He tried to rise quickly but felt a shooting pain, and he realised that he had sprained his ankle. Getting shakily to his feet, he saw Furlong pushing Joe to the ground. With the container in his right hand, Furlong used his left hand to vault over the rail and down onto the deck of the trawler, whose mooring ropes had now been cleared. Tim heard a deep revving from the engine, and the boat started to move away from the quayside. Looking back, he could see that the beggar was trying to rein in the terrified horse amidst the chaos on the flame-covered quayside. Then he saw Joe scrambling to his feet and sprinting along the pier. The *Bailey Maid* was several feet out from the pier now, and Tim could hardly believe his eyes when Joe hurled himself through the air and landed with a thud on the deck of the trawler. Then the vessel suddenly picked up speed and headed for the harbour mouth and the open sea.

CHAPTER SIXTEEN

Deirdre gulped in lungfuls of the salty sea air, as Con Furlong removed her from the carpet and took off her gag. Furlong's brother Mick was at the wheel of the *Bailey Maid*, and the trawler was now far enough from land for them to be out of view of any observer. Deirdre's relief at being able to breathe easily was tempered by disappointment that now Tim and Joe were prisoners also.

All three of them had been made to sit on the deck with their backs to the side of the trawler, and Deirdre's mind was in a whirl as she tried to work out how things might unfold. Even before they had reached the exit from Howth harbour the Furlongs had been in control, with Tim immobilised with a sprained ankle, and Joe knocked to the ground by a blow from Con Furlong.

Now they were steaming towards the horizon, and Furlong stood before them, easily balancing himself as the boat rode the waves. He reached inside his pocket and produced a handgun which he pointed at his three prisoners in turn. Deirdre tried to hide her shock. She knew he was a criminal, but she hadn't expected him to have a gun.

'Just to let you know,' said Furlong, 'this is a Webley revolver. One bullet to the head can blow your brains out. I don't want to have to do that, so don't give me any more trouble.'

Deirdre reckoned that he was trying to frighten them into

submission, and she wasn't sure how to respond. All the odds seemed to be stacked in favour of their captors, with Furlong armed and in control, whereas she was still tied up, and Tim had hurt his ankle. The only possible weapon for fighting back was a knife that Deirdre had noticed thrown on top of a pile of netting. She suspected that the knife was used for gutting fish. If Furlong didn't stay alert, maybe one of the boys could use it to free her. Before she could think about it any further, she was surprised to hear Tim challenging him.

'I don't think you're going to shoot us,' he said.

'Really?'

'People must have seen us getting on your boat. There was such a big kerfuffle – you even left your horse behind.'

'My nephew will take the horse home. And with all the confusion of the fire, people won't be sure what was happening.'

'You'd still have loads of questions to answer if we didn't show up,' said Tim.

Deirdre was impressed by how cool Tim was managing to sound, even though she knew he must be frightened too.

'If need be, we'll brazen that out,' said Furlong. 'But the easier thing is if you stop causing me trouble. Then I can let you go, once we transfer the goods.'

'*The goods?*' said Tim. 'You mean the stolen painting!'

'Call it what you like,' said Furlong. 'Once we transfer it we can return under darkness. We'll dump you, and if you're smart, you'll leave it at that. And thank your lucky stars you're still alive.'

Deirdre tried to weigh up how likely it was that Furlong was telling the truth. Previously he had made the point that if they went to the police, it would be their word against his. And with no evidence he couldn't be convicted. So maybe he really did intend to release them. Then again, she thought nervously, maybe not.

'Just out of curiosity, can I ask one question,' said Joe, speaking for the first time.

'What?'

Joe pointed to the cylindrical container that had been tucked into a coil of rope on the deck. 'What will happen the painting?'

'You needn't worry about that, son,' said Furlong with a crooked grin. 'It'll be in Rotterdam by tomorrow night – and then never seen again in public.'

Deirdre was surprised to hear Furlong speaking so freely. Could that be because he was planning to silence them permanently? Or was he just confident that once the painting vanished in Europe he had nothing to fear?

Furlong looked at the three friends and spoke again. 'In one way I have to admire your guts. But enough's enough. I'm tying you lads up, and you'll stay that way till this is over.'

Furlong pocketed the gun and reached over to pick up some dirty-looking rope from beside the fishing nets. While he was briefly distracted Joe whispered urgently in Deirdre's ear.

'When I cough loudly pretend you're getting sick!'

Before Deirdre had a chance to reply, Furlong had gathered the rope and turned back.

'Hands out,' he said to Tim.

Joe looked enquiringly at Deirdre. She had no idea what he had in mind, but she thought that anything was surely better than being at the mercy of the Furlongs. She swallowed hard, held his gaze, and quickly nodded.

* * *

Joe watched as Furlong began tying Tim's wrists together. He stared at his friend's face, willing Tim to catch his eye. After a moment Tim glanced over, and Joe immediately winked meaningfully. Tim looked back uncertainly as Furlong bent to tie his ankles, and Joe nodded urgently and winked again to covey to his friend that he had something in mind. Tim nodded in reply, then Furlong rose and approached Joe.

Joe had deliberately made his demeanour seem passive, and he meekly held out his hands now. 'Please, don't make it too tight,' he said.

As Furlong held out a length of rope, Joe coughed.

'Oh, no!' cried Deirdre, immediately convulsing, and raising her bound wrists to her mouth. She retched loudly as though vomiting, and Furlong turned towards her. Tim instantly swung his outstretched hands and grabbed for the gun in Furlong's trouser pocket. He got his hand around the handle of the revolver, but to his horror it snagged in the lining of the pocket. Joe wriggled it and pulled again as Furlong swung round to face him. This time the gun came clear of the pocket, and Joe got his finger onto the trigger. Furlong made a grab for the weapon just as Joe swung it round. Joe jerked hard. He had intended to prevent Furlong from disarming him. Instead, the weapon discharged with a deafening bang.

* * *

Tim watched aghast as Furlong tumbled backwards against the side of the boat. He had expected to see the fisherman covered in blood. Now, though, he realised that the shot hadn't hit him, and that Furlong had been pushed backwards by Joe in the struggle for the revolver.

'Get back to the wheel!' shouted Joe to Furlong's brother, who had left his post on hearing the shot. 'No-one was hit. Get back to the wheel!' Joe swung the gun around and aimed it at the man. 'Now!'

Reluctantly he returned to steering the boat, and Joe switched his attention, swivelling around to point the revolver at Con Furlong who was rising to his feet.

'Stay where you are!' he ordered while moving sideways to pick up the knife from the top of the fishing nets.

'Free yourself and Deirdre!' Joe said, quickly crossing back to place the knife in Tim's hands.

Tim gripped the knife as Joe swung round again to cover Furlong with the gun. Cutting his own bound hands was awkward, but to Tim's relief the knife was razor sharp and it cut through the old rope easily. With his wrists free, Tim swiftly cut the rope around his ankles, then leaned over and freed Deirdre's hands and feet.

'Stay back!' shouted Joe, and from the corner of his eye Tim could see that Furlong had moved towards his friend.

'Put the gun down, sonny,' said Furlong slowly advancing.

Tim could see from Joe's face that he didn't want to shoot an unarmed man, and clearly Furlong had sensed it too. Suddenly the fisherman sprang forward, lunging for the weapon. He crashed into Joe, spinning him sideways and knocking the gun from his hand.

Tim saw the revolver falling to the ground and sliding along the deck. Immediately his instincts kicked in, and before he knew what he was doing he rolled over on the deck, reached out his arm and scooped up the gun.

'Back off!' he roared at Furlong. 'Back off or I'll empty this into you!'

'OK! OK! Take it easy.'

Tim's ankle still felt painful, but he hoisted himself to a standing position, all the while pointing the gun at Furlong. 'Move away from him!' he said to Deirdre who had just risen to her feet. His sister obeyed him at once, distancing herself from the trawlerman.

'Tell your brother to turn around and bring us back to Howth,' ordered Tim.

Furlong said nothing for a moment, then shook his head. 'That can't happen.'

'Tell him or I'll use this,' said Tim.

'That's the thing. I don't think you will. I can see it in your eyes. You're a frightened kid – you're not a killer.'

'I can see what's in your eyes too. And you *could* be a killer. And maybe you *would be* if you had the gun.'

'More likely not. But I don't have the gun. You do. Only you're not going to use it, are you?'

'Don't listen to him, Tim!' said Deirdre.

'Oh, but Tim is listening. And he knows I'm telling the truth.'

Tim could feel his hands trembling, but he kept the weapon pointed at Furlong's chest. 'I'll use it if I have to,' he said.

'No. Because, like I said, once we've done the transfer, I'll let you all go.'

'Sure, you will,' said Joe sarcastically.

'And for good measure you'll let my father go to jail,' said Tim, 'for a crime he didn't commit.'

'He hasn't been charged with anything yet,' said Furlong.

'*Yet*,' said Tim.

'Probably never.'

'As if you care.'

'Actually, you're right. I don't care one way or another. So you know what this all boils down to. Have you got the stomach to kill me?'

Tim could feel his trembling getting worse.

'Look at you,' said Furlong. 'You're so out of your depth it's a joke.' He stepped forward and put his hand out. 'Pass it over and no-one gets hurt.'

'Stop!' cried Tim.

'You're not going to kill me.'

'I'll maim you!'

'Don't think so.'

Furlong kept moving forward, and Tim tried to fight down a rising panic. Suddenly Furlong grabbed for the gun. Tim side-stepped. He swung round and raised the gun again, holding it in both hands to try to keep it steady. Then he took aim, pulled the trigger and shot Con Furlong.

* * *

Deirdre fired the distress flare and watched it hanging in the air, its bright red light a contrast to the blue of the sky. She hoped that it would alert other vessels, or better yet, the coastguard, to come to their aid. She looked over to where Con Furlong lay on the deck. His trouser leg was soaked in blood from where Tim had shot him in the thigh. Despite being in obvious pain, she had to admit that he was tough; he grunted and propped himself up then tried to stem the flow of blood with a large handkerchief that he took from his pocket.

'Turn back and head for Howth,' said Tim, pointing the gun at Furlong's brother.

'I don't take orders from kids,' he answered sulkily.

'Forget orders,' said Joe, 'and look at the facts. Your brother is losing blood. The sooner we head back, the sooner he gets treated.'

'Don't mind him, Mick,' said Furlong, 'I can patch it up.'

'Yes, we've only to look at your leg to see what a great job you're doing,' said Deirdre. She walked over to stand behind Mick. 'You've a simple decision here,' she said matter-of-factly. 'You can turn back and save your brother's life. Or you can sail on and watch him slowly bleed to death. Your choice.'

* * *

Joe stood in the bow of the *Bailey Maid*, a warm breeze blowing against his face. The trawler rose and fell, traversing the sparkling blue surface of the water, and Joe felt elated that after all the challenges, they had outsmarted Wilson and the Furlongs. Deirdre's stark choice had got through to Furlong's brother Mick, who had angrily changed course and was now travelling at top speed back to Howth harbour. Furlong had strapped a makeshift tourniquet around his leg to stem the loss of blood, but he still needed medical treatment as soon as possible.

Joe looked back now to see how he was doing. Despite the pain that he must have been feeling he had done no moaning or groaning. He was still a dangerous criminal, but a tiny part of Joe couldn't help but admire the man's refusal to show any signs of weakness. But if Joe's admiration for Furlong was reluctant, he had no such qualms when it came to Deirdre and Tim. Deirdre had always been daring and had shown her courage and resourcefulness all during this adventure. Tim, though, had been more of a revelation. Despite being his best friend, Joe recognised that Tim wasn't as daring and brave as his sister. And yet, when it had come to the crunch, he had come good, facing down Furlong, and doing what he himself had failed to do, and shooting their adversary.

Joe watched his friend now, who was standing behind Mick, gun at the ready, to make sure he didn't deviate from navigating back to port. Deirdre was sitting on the fishing nets and Joe gave her a thumbs-up that she smilingly returned. It was the first time Joe had fully relaxed since running away from the cricket club – which now seemed an age ago. Suddenly the calm atmosphere was shattered. With Furlong suffering from a gunshot wound and loss of blood, Joe had thought of him as posing little further threat. But now Furlong struck unexpectedly. Except this time it wasn't a physical attack. Instead, he quickly reached out and grabbed the cylindrical container that held the painting. In one swinging motion he flung it into the air, over the side of the trawler into the sea.

'Now you've no evidence,' he said. 'No evidence – no case. So you've just shot an innocent man.'

* * *

Deirdre sat stunned on the fishing nets. In her wildest dreams she couldn't have imagined Furlong dumping the highly valuable painting. But he had, and with it went the chance to prove him a criminal, and her father an innocent man. It was a ruthless act of vandalism, but it had a brutal logic. And it meant that after all they had been through, Furlong would emerge the winner. The thought was sickening, and barely knowing what she was doing, Deirdre sprang to her feet. She ran to where Furlong sat propped up on the deck and screamed at him. 'No! You don't get away with that!'

He cowered slightly, taken aback by her fury. He raised his arm as though to shield himself from an attack, but Deirdre went around him. She clambered up onto the rail of the boat, struggling to keep her balance in the swell. She heard Tim and Joe shouting at her to get down, but she blocked them and everything else from her head. *She had to retrieve the painting, or all would be lost.* She paused briefly, gathering her nerve. Then she launched herself forward and dived into the sea.

* * *

For a split-second Tim stood immobile. He was stupefied by Deirdre's move. But another part of his brain recognised that what she had done was their only chance of getting back the painting. Snapping into action himself, he raised the gun and shouted at Mick. 'Turn around! Turn around and pick her up!'

Mick didn't answer at once. Instead, he reached out, grabbed a lifebuoy, and threw it over the side. 'She can swim up to that and wait till she's rescued,' he said. 'We can't waste time circling around. You said yourself, Con needs to get to a doctor.'

'And that's where we're taking him! But first go back for Deirdre!'

'You can point the gun as much as you like,' said Mick. 'But I'm not wasting time while my brother bleeds out. So no, I'm not turning back.'

* * *

Deirdre kicked her legs vigorously and sliced her arms through the water in a fast Australian crawl. She had seen the cylindrical container on the surface of the water when she had stood on the rail of the boat. But there was no telling how long it would stay afloat, and she wanted to reach it as quickly as possible. Despite the June sunshine the deep waters of the Irish Sea felt cold, but she put her own discomfort aside and concentrated on getting to the container. With the swell of the waves it fell from view each time it went into a trough, and Deirdre tried to adjust her direction without losing speed whenever she saw it.

Even as she concentrated on getting to the container, she knew that what she had done was dangerous. She had acted purely on impulse and now she was counting on Tim to get the *Bailey Maid* to turn around and come back for her. He had the gun, she told herself, and that meant that his orders would surely be obeyed. Wouldn't they?

Distracted by her thoughts, she was taken by surprise by a big wave, and she swallowed some water. The salty water tasted horrible, but she fought the urge to gag and spat out the water, then forced herself to put thoughts of Tim and the trawler out of her head. *She had to concentrate on the task in hand*. She was grateful now for the hours she had spent racing with her swimming club, and she put all her energy into slicing through the water at speed. She knew she must be nearing the location of the container, and suddenly it rose before her on the crest of a wave. With a final burst of power she closed the gap and grabbed the leather strap of the container. She felt a surge of satisfaction as she gripped it tightly while threading water. Then she swung about, lifted her head as high as possible, and looked for any sign of the *Bailey Maid*.

* * *

'Turn around!' shouted Tim. 'That's my sister, we're not leaving her!'

'And that's my brother who's losing blood!' answered Mick not looking around from the wheel as the boat ploughed on. 'Your sister can swim to the buoy,' he said. 'She wouldn't have dived in if she wasn't a good swimmer.'

Tim glanced backward, shocked to see how far behind Deirdre was already.

'No!' he cried. 'She mightn't have even seen the buoy. 'Turn the boat right now!'

'Or what? You'll kill me? Who steers the vessel then?'

'Look at me!' shouted Tim. 'Look at me!'

Mick turned around, and Tim aimed the gun at him.

'I won't kill you. But I'll shoot you in the leg too. And you can risk bleeding out as you guide us back to port. I did it to your brother and I'll do it to you. Now turn the boat around!'

Mick said nothing, and Tim realised he was going to try to brazen it out. 'OK,' said Tim, 'if that's how you want it!' He cocked the pistol and aimed it at the man's leg.

'All right!' cried Mick, 'all right!'

Tim kept the gun trained on him, and his finger on the trigger, as Mick swung the wheel sharply and the *Bailey Maid* changed course.

* * *

Deirdre bobbed around in the water, rising and falling with the swell while firmly holding onto the leather strap. She had felt hugely relieved to see the trawler turning back, but now another worry played on her mind. The container had floated on the surface and seemed well-constructed, but supposing seawater had got in and the painting was water-damaged?

Destroyed even? All their efforts would be in vain.

She prayed that wouldn't be the case, then put it from her mind as she saw the *Bailey Maid* approaching. She heard the engine slowing and saw Joe standing in the bow.

'Well done, Deirdre!' he shouted, before throwing her a rope-ladder.

Deirdre swam to where the ladder had landed on the water. She gripped the rope-ladder with one hand, held onto the container with the other, and allowed herself to be pulled to safety.

CHAPTER SEVENTEEN

J oe sat at the front of the coastguard vessel, lost in his thoughts as the boat slowed down, then passed the lighthouse and entered Howth harbour. Sitting beside him was Tim, and on the other side was Deirdre, who was wrapped in a blanket and sipping from a mug of cocoa that one of the crew members had made to warm her up after her time in the sea.

The distress flare had done its job, and the coastguard cutter had sped to their rescue soon after Deirdre had clambered back aboard the *Bailey Maid*. The captain of the coastguard vessel had been amazed to find Tim holding two criminals at gunpoint, but when the full story had been relayed to him, he had acted swiftly.

Con Furlong had been given medical treatment, Mick Furlong placed in handcuffs, and the two fishermen and the three friends had been transferred from the *Bailey Maid* to the faster coastguard vessel. A couple of experienced sailors had been left behind to take the trawler back to port, and Joe realised now that the adventure with his friends was reaching its endgame.

He thought back to the crucial moment when Deirdre had climbed the rope ladder and deposited the cylindrical container on the deck of the trawler.

'Please, God...let it...let it not be ruined,' she had gasped, shaking with the cold and short of breath after her long swim. Tim had been holding the gun on the two Furlongs, and with

Deirdre looking exhausted, Joe felt that the onus was on him.

'Do you want…do you want me to open it and see if the painting's all right?' he asked.

It was the moment he suspected they were all dreading, and he sensed the nervousness of his friends.

'Yes, why don't you?' said Tim.

'Please,' agreed Deirdre.

Joe reached down and took up the container. It was wet on the outside from the seawater, but the cylinder seemed to be well sealed. Yet if water had got in, a highly-valuable painting would be damaged. Worse still, if the painting was ruined beyond recognition their main piece of evidence would be useless, and the case against Wilson and the Furlongs could collapse.

Joe dried the outside of the container with a piece of cloth. Holding his breath, he reached for the two sprung catches that sealed the lid in place. He snapped them open, hesitated briefly, then turned the container upside down. Immediately a rolled-up canvas fell down into his hands. Joe slowly unfurled it. It was the stolen painting, dry and undamaged, and he breathed a huge sigh of relief.

Thinking back on it now, Joe felt a sense of triumph, even if it was slightly galling that he wouldn't get to see Charles Wilson being led away in handcuffs. Still, Deirdre was a direct witness to Wilson delivering the stolen goods to Furlongs cottage, and Joe himself would give sworn testimony, so there seemed little doubt that the gallery director would be convicted, and that Mr Kavanagh would be seen to be completely innocent.

He turned to his friend. 'OK, Tim?'

'Yes. Well…I just…'

'What?'

'I can't believe I shot a man.'

'You had to.'

'I know. But still…'

'No, Tim. No buts. You only wounded him. But you had to. It saved our lives. *You* saved our lives. You're a hero.'

Tim smiled wryly. 'Never thought I'd hear anyone say that.'

Joe grinned. 'You better get used to it.' Just then he felt the engines throttling back. 'OK, here we go,' he said. Then he rose to his feet, eager to see what would happen next as the boat drew up to the pier.

CHAPTER EIGHTEEN

T im could hardly believe his eyes. He was seated with Deirdre and Joe in a large, airy office in Howth police station where he had been taken after the coastguard cutter had docked. Chief Superintendent Leech, the senior police officer overseeing the case of the stolen painting, had arrived in Howth. Clearly delighted to have the valuable painting safely recovered, he had organised lemonade and bowls of ice cream for the three friends, as well as dry clothes for Deirdre.

Now, though, Tim was flabbergasted, and he stopped with a spoon of ice cream halfway to his mouth when he saw who had just entered the room.

Chief Superintendent Leech smiled. 'Let me introduce Detective Constable Hennessy,' he said.

'Oh my goodness!' cried Deirdre, while Tim and Joe stared at Detective Constable Hennessy, lost for words.

He was the beggar who had been sitting on the quayside, only now he had divested himself of some of his ragged clothes.

'Sorry I couldn't intervene sooner at the pier,' he said. 'Though it turns out you did pretty well on your own,' he added with a grin.

'Detective Hennessy has been on observation duty since we got the anonymous letter,' explained Leech. 'I assume that was sent by you.'

Joe nodded. 'Yes. But we thought you weren't taking it seriously.'

'Oh, we took it seriously all right. Detective Hennessy has a sore backside from sitting on the quay for two days. Am I right, Detective?'

'Absolutely, sir.'

'But we had to be extremely cautious,' continued Leech. 'Charles Wilson moves in high circles. To accuse a person like that in the wrong, or without solid evidence, was out of the question.'

Tim didn't want to seem ungrateful for the ice cream and the lemonade, but he had to speak up. 'Whereas our da, he was just a train guard?' he said.

'Your father wasn't *accused*, Tim. He was questioned. Questioned at length, I admit, and I'm sorry he had to go through that ordeal. But he was one of the staff on the train when the painting went missing. If we *hadn't* regarded him as a possible suspect, we wouldn't have been doing our job.'

'It was still awful for him,' said Deirdre.

'I understand that. And like I say, I'm sorry. But all's well that ends well. We have the painting back, undamaged. The Furlong brothers – two gentlemen already known to the force – are in custody. Con Furlong is on his way to hospital under police escort, and Mick Furlong is singing like a canary in the hope of reducing his sentence. And Charles Wilson will be spending tonight in a cell, with the prospect of a stiff sentence when this case comes to court.'

'Good enough for him!' said Tim.

'Indeed,' agreed Chief Superintendent Leech. 'We'll need to take detailed statements from all of you. Meanwhile, your parents will be notified, and we'll transport them out here so they can be with you.'

'I ran out of the cricket club without telling Dad where I was going,' said Joe. 'He'll kill me.'

'I think in the circumstance he probably won't,' said the policeman with a smile. 'I'll smooth it over with him. I know he works for the Midland Great Western Railway, and I'll remind him how grateful the company will be to have the case solved, and the painting returned.'

'Thank you,' said Joe.

'And as for you two,' said Leech, turning back to Tim and Deirdre. 'I think, like your friend here, you're going to be heroes in your neighbourhood.'

'We never…we never set out to be heroes,' said Deirdre. 'We just did what we had to do to clear our da's name.'

'You've still been really clever, and really brave. Well done,' said Chief Superintendent Leech.

'Thanks,' replied Tim, pleased by the policeman's praise.

'Having said that,' added Leech, 'we don't generally encourage heroism. It can end badly. So maybe next time – if there ever *is* a next time – come to us, and don't do it all on your own. All right?'

'Next time – and I hope there *is* a next time – we'll remember that,' said Tim with a smile.

Then he winked at Joe and Deirdre, saluted Chief Superintendent Leech with his spoon, and tucked into his ice cream.

HISTORICAL NOTE

*T*he *Case of the Vanishing Painting* is a work of fiction, and the families of Deirdre, Tim, and Joe are figments of my imagination. Great Western Square, however, is a real place in Dublin, as is Iona Road, where I located Mr Wilson's house.

Howth harbour is still used by trawlers, although its appearance has altered a lot since 1911. The Hill of Howth tramline that features in the story ceased running in 1959, but the wonderful views from the summit and the cliff path are largely unchanged, although Con Furlong's cottage is a fictitious location.

Amiens Street Station had its name changed to Connolly Station in 1966, to honour James Connolly on the fiftieth anniversary of the Easter Rising, while Broadstone railway station, where Mr Kavanagh and Mr Martin worked, closed to passenger traffic in 1937, and today its track bed is used by the Luas tram system.

Phoenix Cricket Club, where Joe and his father played, was founded in 1830 and is the longest-established cricket club in Ireland, and still has its pitch and clubhouse in Dublin's Phoenix Park.

St Peter's Church in Phibsboro, where Mr Martin sang in the choir, is a real church that has one of the highest steeples in Dublin, and although there has been much house-building since

1911, it's still possible to have a picnic on the banks of the River Tolka – as Deirdre, Tim, and Joe did – in one of the linear parks through which the Tolka now flows.

Brian Gallagher,
Dublin 2023

ACKNOWLEDGEMENTS

My thanks to the late Michael O'Brien, who first suggested the idea of a mystery novel set in early twentieth century Ireland, to my editor, Helen Carr, for her superb editing and sound advice, to publicists Ruth Heneghan and Chloe Coome, for all their efforts on my behalf, to Emma Byrne and Dermot Flynn for their sterling work on cover design, and to everyone at O'Brien Press, with whom it's a pleasure to work.

My sincere thanks go to Fingal Arts Office for their bursary support, and to the Arts Council for a Professional Development award.

And finally, my deepest thanks are for the constant encouragement of my family, Miriam, Orla, Mark, Holly, Max, Peter, and Shelby.

Growing up with

tots to teens and in between

Why CHILDREN love O'Brien:

Over 350 books for all ages, including picture books, humour, fiction, true stories, nature and more

Why TEACHERS love O'Brien:

Hundreds of activities and teaching guides, created by teachers for teachers, all FREE to download from obrien.ie

Visit, explore, buy
obrien.ie